Adam's Starling

'Perdue's handling of the Adam/Grandad scenes are not only brilliant, they are also genuinely moving, and the starling plot is never allowed to become tweety-sweety. My nine-year-old thought it fantastic'
Niall MacMonagle, The Irish Times

'*Adam's Starling* belongs on the shelf of any home with school-going children ... The bonding-with-animals theme makes this an appealing book, crashing through age and gender definitions in a warm-hearted way'
Evening Herald

'A gentle novel which confronts a serious problem in a sensitive and honest way'
Judges of the Eilís Dillon Award 2002

'An extremely thought-provoking book that would be an easy read for most 9- to 11-year-olds'
Inis, Children's Books in Ireland magazine

ADAM'S STARLING

GILLIAN PERDUE

Illustrated by Barry Reynolds

THE O'BRIEN PRESS
DUBLIN

First published 2001 by The O'Brien Press Ltd,
20 Victoria Road, Dublin 6, Ireland.
Tel: +353 1 4923333; Fax: +353 1 4922777
E-mail: books@obrien.ie
Website: www.obrien.ie
Reprinted 2002, 2005.

ISBN: 0-86278-685-1

British Library Cataloguing-in-Publication Data
Perdue, Gillian
Adam's Starling
1.Starlings - Juvenile fiction
2.Human-animal relationships - Juvenile fiction
I.Title II.Reylods, Barry
823.9'14[J]

3 4 5 6 7 8 9
05 06 07 08 09

The O'Brien Press receives
assistance from

Editing, layout, typesetting, design: The O'Brien Press Ltd
Illustrations: Barry Reynolds
Printing: Cox & Wyman Ltd

CONTENTS

For Jessie and Sara

Acknowledgements

I would like to thank Liz Morris for constant encouragement and Adrienne Perdue for further encouragement plus typing! Thank you, also, to Eilís French and Íde ní Laoghaire for their hard work and skilful editing and to Lynn Pierce in the art department and Barry Reynolds for the lovely illustrations. A huge thank you to fourth class, Rathfarnham Parish National School and their teacher, Ian Packham, for test-reading. A final thank you to Angus, the Enabler!

1

GRANDAD

The old man sat close by the window, staring out through the grimy glass. He was wearing a heavy jumper, though the hospital room was warm and stuffy.

As Adam came in, the old man turned and looked excitedly at him. 'Did you get the paper? We'll be off soon, won't we?'

Adam grinned and nodded. 'Sure did. Here you are.' He handed his grandfather the evening paper. 'How are you, Grandad?' he asked, dragging a chair across from the central table and sitting down beside the old man.

'Fine, fine. I'm fine,' Grandad replied, shifting

in his chair and pulling the blanket up further on his lap. 'Fine. Grand,' he repeated, gazing out the window.

Then he turned and looked directly at Adam with watery blue eyes. 'Did you not bring your coat, or something to keep warm?'

'Keep warm?' echoed Adam. 'But it's roasting in here –'

The old man continued without waiting for him to finish. 'It'll be a long journey, you know. And they never heat these trains properly.'

Adam smiled and sat back in the hard hospital chair. Now he knew what was on Grandad's mind. It had been a while since they'd had the one where they went on the train. This would be fun.

'Nah, I'm not cold,' he said with a grin. 'I think the train's warm enough. Just perfect.'

The old man nodded, then seemed to lose interest in the conversation and began leafing through the newspaper. His lips moved as he read. Adam sat quietly beside him.

It really was stuffy in the room, and the air was

stale. Adam got up. 'Grandad? Do you mind if I open the window just a little?' He headed towards the window, intending to open the smaller one at the top.

'Sit down, son!' Grandad said urgently. 'Are you mad? You'll lose your seat.'

Adam sat down with a little smile. He'd forgotten that: Grandad was always worried that they wouldn't get seats, or that they might lose the ones they had. He looked around the room, wondering how his grandfather could possibly think he was on a train.

They were in the day ward of a geriatric hospital. There was a large central table which was where the patients had their meals. Arranged around the sides of the room were armchairs and wheelchairs, with smaller tables and magazine racks between them. This ward usually held seven or eight elderly people. Adam's grandad always sat in the chair by the window.

Though the room housed seven adults, it was strangely quiet. They didn't talk much. Some dozed, or sat leafing through magazines or books. Over in one corner sat a rake-thin old man whom the staff called Birdy. He never spoke, but he whistled constantly – little chirps and tweets that sounded exactly like birdsong. One old lady held the remote control for the TV, which she watched with the volume turned way down. Many were lost in their own worlds, like Adam's grandad, who had no idea he was in hospital. Some days he would think he was at home, though he hadn't lived there for over a year, since Adam's granny had died. Other times, he thought he was waiting in the doctor's surgery, or, like today, that he was on a train. Adam liked the train best. His grandad was fairly alert on those days, looking forward to a day at the beach or a weekend trip.

Adam reached into his jacket pocket and pulled out a bag of Maltesers and a bar of chocolate. Grandad had a sweet tooth. 'I brought sweets for the trip, Grandad,' he said, placing them on the old man's lap.

'Great, great!' exclaimed Grandad, with a

gleeful expression as he picked them up. 'Thanks, son!' He often called Adam 'son'; Adam did look very like his Uncle Gary had when he was nine. But Gary was in his forties now and lived in Australia. He was a long way from the boy he'd once been. Grandad had three daughters as well – Adam's mother, Deirdre, was one.

As if on cue, Adam heard his mam coming down the corridor; she'd been parking the car. The heels of her boots clicked on the floor and she swished into the room, bringing a blast of cool air from outside with her.

'Hi, Dad.' She marched briskly over to the old man and bent to kiss him. Grandad reared back in his seat, away from the embrace. 'Madam!' he exclaimed loudly. 'I don't even know you! Please!'

Deirdre stepped back and looked questioningly at Adam, who shrugged. 'He thinks I'm Gary today,' he whispered to her, 'and it's the train.'

Deirdre stood helplessly, two coins of colour appearing high up on her cheeks, as Grandad continued loudly: 'All these seats are taken, my

good woman. I'm afraid you'll have to sit somewhere else.'

She glanced in embarrassment at the other
patients and began pulling a chair over from the
group at the table, but by now Grandad was
finding the stranger's persistence irritating.
'Madam,' he snapped, 'I'm trying to have a quiet
chat with my son. There really is no room in this
carriage.'

Deirdre sighed and put the chair back. It was
going to be one of those days!

The old man relented a little. 'Perhaps if you try
further down the train,' he said kindly. 'There's
usually space in the back.' He turned to Adam
with a sly smile. 'Now, let's admire the scenery
and enjoy the goodies!' he whispered mischievously.

Grandad and Adam sat munching chocolate in
companionable silence, and staring out the
window. Adam saw a scruffy patch of grass, which
was leaf-strewn and needed cutting. Behind it was
a small car park, and behind that again was the

main hospital. Adam glanced at his grandfather, wondering what he saw.

'Would you like me to get you anything to drink, Grandad?' The last time they'd played this game, Adam had got a cold drink and cups of tea from the small café down the corridor.

Grandad was still gazing out the window. 'Hmm?' he murmured, turning towards Adam.

'They have a restaurant car on this train, Grandad. I can get you a cup of tea if you like.'

'That'd be nice, son. In a little while, maybe. We've a long way to go, you know.'

Behind them, at the table, Deirdre leafed through *Hello* magazine and sighed. Adam took off his sweatshirt and tied it around his waist. His gaze caught Birdy's across the room. Adam blew his hair off his forehead and fanned himself. 'It's roasting, isn't it?' he called to the frail old man.

'Tweet-tweet, tweet-tweet-tweet!' chirruped Birdy by way of reply.

* * *

The next afternoon, Adam wasn't quite so warm. His feet were soaking. He could feel the seams of his socks pressing into his cold, clammy toes. He had been in such a rush to get out of school that he'd forgotten the enormous puddle lying in wait just outside the school entrance. He'd been zipping up his jacket, half-running, half-walking, when – *splash!* – he'd gone straight into it. As if that weren't bad enough, he'd only gone a few more squelchy steps when a passing car whizzed through another puddle on the road, drenching him all down one side. *Great!* thought Adam. *Just great!*

He walked past the side of the school, and then – *blam!* Something smacked him hard on the back of the head.

He looked down. At his feet was a carton of school milk; that was what had hit him. It had burst, and milk seeped out onto the path, forming a white map of Italy on the ground.

'Hey! A-A-Adam!' yelled a voice. A stocky boy with close-cropped brown hair was running towards him. It was PJ, a kid from Adam's class. A not-very-nice kid from his class. 'I'm going to tell the teacher you're robbing milk out of the school.'

He was joined by another boy, skinny and freckle-faced, with the look of a whippet. They stopped a few feet from Adam, grinning and sniggering. Adam began slowly backing away.

Shane, the skinny one, shouted, 'Yeah! And I'll tell her you've been bursting the cartons, too. You're in for it!'

'W-wait! Sh-Shane!' stammered Adam. 'That's n-not fair.' He shifted from one squelching foot to the other, unsure whether he should reason with them or just run for it.

He didn't have much time to decide. Rory, Shane's twin, a lankier, scrawnier version of his brother, came running up to the others, clutching four or five cartons of milk. He doled them out.

'You'd better leg it, Addy-waddy!' he sniggered. 'These milks are from last week! I found them behind the bins.'

Adam knew he had to do something. He picked up the now-empty milk carton that had hit him and threw it at the three boys. It drifted sadly through the air and landed at Shane's feet with a sorrowful *plock*.

'Brutal!' said PJ.

'Pathetic!' sneered Shane.

'You can't even throw, you sap!' yelled Rory, hurling not one carton, but two at Adam.

Adam turned to run, but it was too late. A milk carton caught him right on the shoulder and he was splattered all over the face and neck with foul-smelling, lumpy, sour milk. A second carton whacked into his schoolbag and milk began dripping down the sides, into all the nooks and crannies, and seeping slowly through the zip. The smell was disgusting.

Adam hastily wiped the worst of it off his face and ran as fast as he could towards the main road. As his feet pounded the path, he bit back hot tears of rage and humiliation. *Just let me get away from them – just let me get away,* he thought.

He ran on, over the bank and down to the verge of the main road. Across the road, at the bus shelter, he could see his cousin Danny waiting for him, laughing and talking with two teenage girls.

Danny was eighteen. He had left school and was doing a training course in the mornings at the local vocational college; he wanted to be a chef. He met Adam most days after school and spent the afternoons with him. He was meant to be minding Adam until six o'clock, when Deirdre got back from work – but, to Adam, it never felt like he was being minded. He really liked Danny, though he thought he looked all wrong for a chef. For a start, he was thin and very tall. He was also blond, with an earring and a permanent grin. He had a black biker's jacket, which he wore summer and winter alike. His friends and family poked fun at both his height and his lack of padding, calling him Lanky Lout or Stick Insect, but Danny just grinned even more.

When Danny came into your house, the first thing he'd say was: 'Any nosh? Anything decent to eat?' He was always starving. 'That's why I want to be a chef,' he said, 'so's I'll always have plenty of grub!' When Danny smiled, you found yourself grinning foolishly back at him – you couldn't help it. Adam had often wished he could be like his big cousin.

The sight of Danny calmed him a bit. He paused, gasping, and allowed himself to turn around. There was no sign of Rory and Shane. PJ was a good way off, heading across the football pitch, in the opposite direction.

Adam sighed in relief, wiped his face again, and crossed over to Danny.

'Hey, Adam!' Danny shot a wink and a half-grin in the general direction of the two girls, by way of farewell. As Adam approached, the grin faded.

'What the ...?' He stared at Adam, at his flushed face and milk-sodden coat. 'What happened? Look at the state of you!' Danny winced as the smell reached him.

Adam shook his head. He didn't trust himself to speak.

Danny waited a moment. 'Come on,' he said. 'We'll head home. You can tell me on the way.'

Adam was almost running to keep up with Danny's long strides, but it was easier to talk now that they were doing something else.

'It ... it was just some of the lads at school,' he began.

'No!' exclaimed Danny. 'Well, I didn't think you'd taken a milk shower all by yourself. Who did it? Did the teachers nab them?'

Adam shook his head. 'They ran off.'

'Of course they did.' Danny snorted. 'I wish I'd been there ... I'll sort it for you, Adam. Who was it?'

Adam said nothing. He was tempted to tell, but he was scared of what would happen if he did. And there was something else. He was ashamed – ashamed and annoyed with himself for doing nothing. *They're right*, he thought. *I am a sap.*

Danny was still waiting for an answer.

'I'll be fine, Danny,' said Adam without conviction. 'I'll sort it myself.'

Danny sighed in frustration. 'Well, if you need me, you know where I am.'

Adam managed a small 'Thanks' as they walked on – Danny striding, Adam squelching and stinking.

2

TROUBLE AT SCHOOL

Adam stood looking at himself in the bathroom mirror. Though he'd washed his hair about ten times the night before, he still imagined he could smell the sour milk. He leaned close to the cool glass until his nose was touching it, and sniffed ... nah, it must be gone.

Sighing, he stepped back and searched his face for a clue, some reason that would explain the bullying. Maybe there was something wrong with him. Maybe he looked too stupid ... maybe he looked too clever ... there had to be something!

But all he saw was an even, ordinary face: blue eyes, brown hair cut nice and spiky at the back.

Sometimes, when he'd just got his hair cut, Mam would say, 'Come here till I feel your hair,' and Adam would stand really still while she rubbed his hedgehog hair. He loved that ... What else? He saw freckles; a small red scar from a fall when he was a toddler; normal ears, not too sticky-out ... He saw an ordinary nine-year-old boy. Just a boy.

'Adam!' a voice called up the stairs. Then, louder, '*Adam*!' He shook his head and blinked, waking himself up, then went out.

Deirdre was in a hurry. She was waiting at the bottom of the stairs, holding Adam's coat. Her long hair was trapped under the collar of her jacket in the way that always irritated her. She had a small M of worry-lines over her nose. That meant she was cross, or about to be cross.

'Come on – get your schoolbag. Have you got your lunch?' She grabbed her handbag from where it hung on the banisters.

Adam ran down the stairs and picked up his schoolbag. He stood in the hall, not wanting the day to begin. Why couldn't he just go back to bed?

Dad appeared on the landing. 'See you later, son,' he called down.

Adam managed to give his dad a smile. 'See you, Dad. Sleep well.'

Adam's dad, Jim, worked night shifts at a computer software firm, which was in an industrial estate about two miles away. Adam hated him doing nights, because it meant that he was often still asleep when Adam got back from school. There was only a short time in which they could see each other before Dad was gone again. Some days, if Adam was late getting back with Danny, he didn't get to see his dad at all.

'Ah, Adam!' snapped Deirdre, exasperated. 'Hurry up. Put your jacket on!' Adam hastily did as she said and they got into the car, ready for the drive to school.

The school was only about five minutes away, if there was no traffic and if all the lights were green. But most mornings there were loads of cars on the road – all in a hurry, all full of people yawning and looking narky – so the drive usually took fifteen or even twenty minutes. Long enough to sit at red lights three times. Long enough to look across at the bridge in the park. Long enough to think about school and to begin feeling bad. Long enough to get the pain.

'Mam, I think I'm sick,' began Adam.

But this morning his mam was having none of it. 'Ah, now listen, Adam. Don't start.' She sounded very firm.

'But –'

Deirdre spoke over him, through gritted teeth. 'Adam, don't even go there. Not today.' She softened her tone slightly and went on, 'Not today, love. You're grand. You'll be fine when you get to school.'

Normally Adam knew to drop it when his mam was in this humour, but the memory of the sour-milk incident made him desperate. He had to try one last time. He clutched his stomach with both hands and arranged his face into the tortured grimace that he thought would go with acute appendicitis. 'But I really do feel bad, Ma, I do,' he whispered.

Deirdre adjusted her driving-mirror so that she could see his face. Her steely blue eyes bored into his. 'Adam, *you – have – to – go – to – school!*' She spoke slowly and clearly, as if he didn't understand English. 'Now, stop your nonsense!' she said in her normal voice. Then she moved the mirror back and turned on the radio. She began to sing along with it.

Adam gave up. That was that.

He sighed and sat back in his seat. They were stopped at the traffic lights. He turned his head to look out the window. High up on a wire was a small, scruffy-looking bird. As Adam looked, the bird turned its head and seemed to look right down into the car.

Then the lights changed and the car moved off. The bird took off too. Adam tried to see where it went, but they passed under a footbridge and he lost sight of it.

They stopped again near the turn-off for the shopping centre. Adam was looking out the window at a circus poster when he saw the same little bird land on the signpost. It had to be the same bird – the gusts of wind caught its feathers, giving it that scruffy look it had had on the wire. Now that he was closer, Adam could see that the bird was greenish-black, with speckles. It looked cheeky and dishevelled, as if it were saying, 'Well, the others may want to waste time preening and washing, but not me. That's a mug's game!'

The little bird cocked its head, looked right into the car at Adam – and winked!

When the car pulled up in front of the school gates, Adam saw Rory and Shane running in ahead of him. They were usually late, so that meant he was even later. He grabbed his bag and pushed the front seat forward.

'Go on, love!' said his mam as he hesitated. 'It'll be fine. Hurry up – you're late.' She gave him a quick kiss and banged the passenger door shut.

'See you later!' called Adam as he ran in the gates and up the path. He began the Prayer for Late Mornings. *Don't let them have gone into the hall already! Please don't let Assembly have started!* There was nothing worse than going into the hall when all the kids were already there, standing in their lines, messing and talking, looking at everyone coming in. Some of the sixth class even slagged any teacher who was late in. 'Ooh! Did you sleep it out, Miss? Very naughty! You should go to bed earlier!'

Adam's prayer worked. His class had only begun to get into a line at the door of the classroom, so he hung up his jacket, dumped his bag at his desk and quickly got into line.

'Hiya, Adam!' said his friend Niamh, turning and flashing him a grin as he lined up behind her. Niamh had long brown hair, which she wore in plaits – she had the longest plaits of all the girls in fourth class. She was tall for her age and could be friendly or fierce, depending on how much she liked you.

Rory was ahead of them in the line. He turned round and gave Adam a push. Adam stumbled out of line, caught off balance.

'Hey!' exclaimed Adam.

'Get into line, Adam,' jeered Rory. 'You're last! Too busy kissing your Mammy? Bye, Mammy!' he mimicked. A few of the others joined in the laughter.

Adam sighed and rejoined the line, saying nothing. Now he really did have a pain in his stomach.

In Assembly they sang a song about winter weather and frosty mornings. The little ones loved it and did all the actions; Adam smiled to see them jumping around and rubbing their hands. Then the principal spoke for a while about football practice and something to do with a swimming gala that was coming up. Adam wasn't really listening until she started on about staying in at break. Some of the kids had been saying they had colds and weren't allowed out. From now on, you would only be allowed to stay in if you were sick – and even then, you needed a note. Adam felt the swirling sickness in his stomach begin for real at the mention of break.

He was getting to hate that word. Break was the

worst time of all – half an hour outside, with all the shoving and pushing and jeering. It wouldn't be too bad if the grass was dry enough for soccer; then Shane and PJ and Rory would forget about him and play football. Or maybe, even better, it would pour rain and they'd have to stay inside. The teachers would stay in too, and your chances of survival improved distinctly if the teacher was in the room.

It's really cloudy, Adam tried to convince himself. He thought about the grey clouds he'd seen on his way to school. *Yeah – it'll definitely be raining by break.* He saw in his mind's eye the hills, the grey clouds and, in front, the telegraph wires with the starling – the starling that had winked at him.

The thought of the bird's inky-black eyes and scruffy feathers made Adam smile. He followed the rest of the line as they jostled and shoved their way back to class, a small smile still at the corner of his mouth.

During the morning, Adam groaned inwardly as he watched the grey sky begin to clear. By break-time, it looked fairly certain that they'd be going outside.

Adam tried to remember what his dad had said about the teasing. 'They're only trying to get a chase off you and annoy you, Adam. Tell them to get lost!' Then he'd leaned towards Adam's ear and whispered, 'Or, better still, trip them up when no one's looking!'

'Ah, Jim! For God's sake!' Mam had overheard.

'Do you know what, Adam?' Dad had said with a grin. 'Your mother has supernatural hearing. She's got ears like a hawk. Well, like a hawk's eyes.' He had put his arm around her then, but Deirdre was having none of it. She clicked her tongue irritably at her husband.

'They have to tell the teacher nowadays, Jim. They can't just trip up the other lad. Adam will be in worse trouble if he does that.' She'd turned to Adam, lifting his chin between her cool fingers so that he looked at her. 'Adam, you have to tell them to leave you alone, and then don't mind them. They're only kids.'

They're only kids. Adam kept repeating the thought as the back door was opened and the screaming children surged outside for break. He decided to go round by the Infants' yard; his friends Niamh and Conor often went there to talk. Adam stuffed his half-eaten sandwich in the bin and headed down the path towards the yard.

What he hadn't seen, though, was PJ running ahead and lurking behind a wall, just out of sight. As Adam turned the corner, he felt a sharp kick to his ankle, followed by a shove. He lost his balance and fell forwards, breaking his fall by grabbing the jacket of a small boy in front of him. Thomas, who was only four, and Adam, who was a medium-sized nine, tumbled in a heap on the hard tarmac.

PJ snorted with laughter and looked around for the teacher on duty. Spying her a few metres away, he shouted loudly in her direction: 'Adam! Adam! Get off Thomas. Stop pulling him down!'

The teacher heard the commotion and turned to see what was going on. Adam was struggling to get up, but from a distance it looked very different.

'Miss! Miss!' yelled PJ again. The teacher began walking briskly over to them.

'Miss,' PJ said eagerly. 'Thomas was only standing there, doing nothing wrong, and Adam came running round the corner and knocked him on the ground! Then he reefed his jacket!' He paused to let this sink in. 'For no reason!' he added in triumph.

The teacher stood surveying the crime scene. Thomas was trying hard not to cry. He looked up at Adam with watery eyes, then noticed the large rip in his coat. 'Waah!' he began to wail. 'Me ma will kill me! That jacket was only new ... Waah!'

PJ leaned against the wall. He was really enjoying this.

'Adam Smith! How do you explain this?' the teacher snapped. 'Never mind, Thomas, we'll get it sorted.' She took Thomas's hand. 'Well, Adam?'

Adam stood up, feeling his cheeks flush, and began: 'Eh, I was only going around the c-corner and then h-he –'

'Look,' interrupted the teacher crossly, 'maybe

it was an accident, but you should be more careful!' She examined the tear in the jacket and continued, 'You'll have to take Thomas's jacket home tonight and get your mum to help you sew it up. And be sure to tell her that it was you who tore it!' she finished. She marched off, with Thomas in tow.

'Yeah! That's r-r-right, Adam. You're a very bold boy,' sneered Rory, who had slunk out from behind a tree to join them. 'Isn't he, PJ?'

PJ nodded vigorously, eyes fixed on his hero, Rory.

'And what do we do with bold boys?' prompted Rory.

'Oh, yeah!' PJ understood: he curled his fist tight and gave Adam a quick, hard punch on the shoulder. It hit the nerve, as it was meant to, and gave Adam a dead arm.

'Yeah,' grinned PJ. 'We'll tell on you, Adam. We'll tell your ma just how bad you are! You'll be dead when she hears she has to fix that coat!'

They ran off, sniggering.

3

STARLINGS

Adam sat at his desk, rubbing the bruise on his shoulder and staring out the window. He could see the soccer pitch and half of the playground. Down on the tarmac, there were seagulls swooping and flapping as they fought over the crusts, broken biscuits and mashed crisps that, as always, littered the playground when the children had gone in. Beside Adam's window there were what seemed like hundreds of small brown birds, pecking at the grass. Chirps and tweeting sounds made their way through the dusty glass and into the silent classroom. They reminded Adam of Birdy, in the home with Grandad.

Adam was gazing idly at the birds, wondering

why the seagulls never came up this close to the window, when he realised that these birds were the same as his bird – the one he'd seen on his way to school. They seemed a bit bigger and smoother-looking, but they were definitely the same kind.

'Excuse me, Miss,' began Adam. He could have kicked himself. Why on earth had he started this?

Miss Hill turned, smiling. 'Yes, Adam?'

It was very quiet in the classroom. Miss Hill waited for him to continue.

'Um, I was just wondering ...' He paused, hating the silence in the room.

'Yes?'

'Wondering what you c-call those birds ...' Adam trailed off lamely. By now, everyone was looking at him and then at each other, sniggering. A sudden flush of heat came to his face and neck. He looked down at his copybook. 'Nothing,' he muttered.

'It's all right, Adam,' said Miss Hill, coming over to his desk. She stood behind him and gave his head a quick pat as she leaned over to look out the window. 'You were asking about those birds? Those are starlings. They're very common, and they probably have nests in the eaves of the school building.'

'What are they eating?' asked Niamh.

'Well, does anyone think they could answer that?' Miss Hill asked.

'Yeah, I know, Teacher,' interrupted Rory. 'They're looking for nuts and Adam's the biggest nut they could find.' There was a general laugh from the back of the classroom.

'That's enough, Rory!' snapped Miss Hill sharply. 'They're eating grass seed, probably, as some new grass was put down a few days ago. Now, perhaps we could all get on with our work, please. Especially you, Rory!' She turned on her heel and walked back to her desk. Rory Brennan was an awful pain at times. Sometimes Miss Hill wished she could answer for Adam and tell Rory to shut up.

'STARLING,' Adam wrote on his copy. Then again, '*starling*,' in joined writing. *It's a nice word,* he thought – *a nice name for a bird.*

He remembered how Grandad, before he was sick, had loved feeding the birds in the park near where he lived. He and Adam would take a big bag of bread and dole it out at the side of the river – some for the ducks and the timid moorhens, some flung into the air for the greedy seagulls to catch in mid-flight, some crumbled onto the dusty path near the bushes for the thrushes, blue-tits and blackbirds. Nana would be furious when they got back – Granddad was meant to use only stale bread, but he usually took whatever he could find. 'Lord Bountiful!' she'd snort, before adding more gently, 'Well, at least you've a good heart.'

Adam decided that the next time he visited the hospital, he'd tell Grandad about the starling. Maybe Birdy knew how to make starling noises ...

Suddenly he felt the jab of a pointy elbow in his ribs. 'Get on with your work,' hissed Niamh urgently. 'Miss Hill's watching you!'

'Okay. Thanks,' whispered Adam, going back to the question he'd been on.

At second break, when most of the boys were playing football, Adam made his way down onto the tarmac and sat on a low bench, facing the school building. He could see the eaves, where the wall and roof of the school met. A strip of wood ran right along there and when he looked closely, Adam could see smallish holes here and there in the wood. As he watched, a starling flew right into one of the holes and disappeared. A few moments later, another darted out from a hole further along.

All through break, Adam sat watching the comings and goings of the little birds. He'd never noticed them before. He couldn't believe how quickly they darted in and out of the eaves.

When the bell rang, the children lined up with all the usual shoving, jostling and pushing. Even before they had left the yard, some of the braver seagulls were swooping to snatch crusts left lying on the tarmac.

Adam moved in the line, heading towards the back door of the school, still watching the starlings. As he passed the eaves, a small movement caught his eye. The little scruffy starling was back, perched on the edge of the gutter, looking down at Adam. Something about the angle of his tiny head made it look as though he was asking a question.

Adam put his hand in his pocket and brought out the remains of a biscuit. He quickly crumbled it and dropped the gritty pieces on the ground. He kept on walking with the others, but just before the line turned the corner he looked back. The starling had flown down and was pecking daintily at the unexpected feast. Adam grinned and went inside.

At home-time, Danny had come right up to the school gates; he was leaning there with his head back, enjoying a weak ray of winter sunshine. He caught Adam's eye and smiled.

'Yo! Adam!' he called. 'I thought I'd come up to the gate today and see your pals.' He strode over to Adam. 'See if the kids are friendly round here,' he continued. 'I wouldn't want anyone giving my cuz a hard time ...' He scanned the faces of the kids as they raced out of the gates. 'Where are the ones that threw the milk at you? Do you want me to talk to them?'

Adam panicked. That would only make things worse. 'No! I'm fine!' he hissed, looking at the ground. 'Leave it.'

'No prob,' said Danny. 'But if you change your mind, or if they're annoying you again, you just tell me. I'll sort it.' He punched Adam's shoulder playfully. 'Danny the Terminator, that's me!'

'Thanks,' said Adam. It was tempting, but only in a fairy-story sort of way: your big cousin comes along and scares the living daylights out of the bullies, they go running off and never come back ... Adam knew things didn't happen like that. He didn't want Danny to do anything. He knew that Rory would just get him later, when Danny wasn't around. Which was all day in school.

'Thanks,' Adam repeated, 'but no thanks.' He decided to change the subject. 'I'm starving. Can we go up to the diner?'

Most evenings Danny worked in an American-style diner with red plastic-covered booths and a mini-jukebox at each table. He and Adam often called in there in the afternoon, to scrounge some food. They headed up there now.

As the boys went in the door, a smiling girl with short blond hair looked up from the table she'd been wiping.

Danny struck his chest and dropped to his knees on the black-and-white-chequered floor. 'What a vision of loveliness! What beauty!' He turned to Adam. 'Did you ever spy such a maiden fair?'

The lovely maiden flung the wet dishcloth at her beloved. 'Shut up, you big eejit!' She grinned at Adam. 'Hiya.'

'Hi,' Adam replied, sitting down on one of the plastic seats.

'We are here to dine, lovely Linda,' continued Danny, getting up off the floor and hopping in behind the tall counter. He peered through the hatch that connected the service area to the kitchen. 'Is your man around?'

Linda shook her head. The boss was a nice enough guy, but he wouldn't want Danny and Adam hanging around clogging up the diner.

'Brill!' exclaimed Danny, licking his lips. 'Any chance of some grub, then, my lovely? Please?'

Linda sighed. Danny decided on a different tack.

'Ah, come on, Linda!' he whined. 'D'ya mean to tell me there isn't a scrap of burger, or even the thinnest little slivers of a few chips, left for my poor starving little cousin?' He jerked his thumb in Adam's direction. 'Look at the state of the little fella! At school all day on his own. And no mammy there to mind him when he comes home.' He grabbed Linda by the waist and swung her round to face Adam. 'Go on!' he hissed at Adam. 'Look cute and hungry!'

Adam rolled his eyes and clutched his stomach.

'Ah, for Pete's sake!' Linda burst out laughing. 'Okay, okay! I'll give you a burger. Just don't roll your eyes like that, Adam! You look sick, not hungry!'

Linda handed the boys two burgers and shoved

them out the door. 'What time are you in later?' she asked Danny, as they headed out.

'Seven o'clock, dearest!' he replied, blowing her an elaborate kiss. 'See you then.'

It was too cold to hang around outside. Music and warm air wafted invitingly from the shopping centre, so Adam and Danny strolled inside, contentedly munching their burgers as they walked.

'Well? Do you like her?' asked Danny.

'Like who?'

'Linda, the lovely Linda who gave us the burgers!' laughed Danny.

Adam nodded. 'She's really nice. Is she your girlfriend?'

'Absolutely! Well, kind of. She's a great girl. She's fun to work with – we have lots of laughs.'

They stopped outside the window of a women's fashion shop, still eating. Danny looked in at the window display of tall, pale shop-dummies arranged in various poses. They were dressed in the latest clothes and stood like beautiful, stern creatures from another planet. They gazed into the distance. Sad, gorgeous, frozen.

'Hey, Adam!' said Danny suddenly. 'Look at the state of these girls! Don't they look like they're starving?'

He pointed at the nearest one, blond with dark-red lips, wearing a grey skirt and jacket. 'Missus! Hey, Missus!' he shouted at the model. 'Does nobody feed you? Here – would you like a bite of my burger?' Adam laughed at the sight of Danny pressing his burger up against the shop window, talking all the while to the dummy. 'Maybe one of your friends would like a bite. Forget the diet, girls, Danny's here!'

Adam was laughing helplessly, doubled over. People were beginning to look and one little girl stopped, dragging her mother by the hand.

'Why's that man talking to the moggles?' she asked, pointing over at Danny.

'He's just having a joke,' said her mum. 'Now, come on!' They carried on, though Adam could see that the mother was chuckling to herself.

'Well, I don't know what's wrong with you,' went on Danny to his blond model. 'I'm a chef – why don't you come over to my place later and I'll fix you a delicious meal? You're way too skinny!'

'Danny, you've really lost it this time,' said Adam, shaking his head and trying to look serious. 'We'd better get you to a doctor. Maybe Grandad's fella would look after you. You're worse than him!' Then, as he spotted a security guard coming over, Adam's smile vanished and he hissed urgently, 'Danny! Come on!'

The security guard had broken into a run – well, more of a shuffling, panting trot – and was trying to talk to someone on his walkie-talkie at the same time. Danny turned and popped the last bit of burger into his mouth just as the red-faced guard reached them.

'What's going on here?' blustered the guard. 'Stop that carry-on or I'll have you thrown out!'

'Commander, I'm very sorry,' said Danny seriously. 'We didn't mean to cause any problems.' He sounded so believable, Adam was nearly convinced. 'My colleague and I' – he pointed at Adam, who was biting his lip, trying not to laugh – 'we are terribly concerned about the state of those poor women. Look at them!' Almost involuntarily, the guard looked in the shop window at the display. 'Dangerously thin, they are!' went on Danny. 'And probably exhausted from standing all day. Do they not have a union? They should think about joining the union –'

'Very funny!' said the guard dryly. 'Ha-blooming-ha! Now, you and your little colleague better get going before I happen to notice the bits of food on that window!' He glanced over at the greasy-looking glass.

'Oops! Better go!' grinned Danny quickly, grabbing Adam's arm and running towards the nearest exit. Adam ran to keep up, though it's not easy to run when you're laughing your legs off.

DANNY

As they walked back home, Danny whistled and hummed fragments of various songs, hands in pockets, lanky legs taking large strides. Adam walked quickly beside him, glancing up every now and then, sometimes jogging for a bit to keep up.

'That was a laugh, wasn't it?' Danny asked. Adam nodded.

'Listen,' said Danny suddenly, 'do you want to come out on Saturday with me and Linda? We'll bring you to see *Alien Empire* if you like.'

Great! was Adam's first thought. He'd been asking his mam for weeks if he could go to *Alien Empire*. 'Thanks, Danny. That'd be brilliant.'

Then a thought struck him. 'But what about you and Linda?' he began.

'Me and Linda?' echoed Danny. 'What about me and Linda? I'd like to see the movie, she'd like to see the movie, Adam would like to see the movie ... Is there a problem?'

Adam could feel a flush beginning at his neck and spreading across his cheeks. He took a deep breath. 'Won't you two be, like ... well ... on a date?'

Danny stopped walking and turned to face Adam. He whacked himself across the forehead and exclaimed in horror, 'Oh my *God*! How could I forget? You're right, Adam. You're absolutely right. I'd forgotten!'

Around them, people elbowed and jostled their way past. Danny placed his hands on Adam's shoulders for emphasis. 'Adam, thanks for reminding me. Of course: Linda is my girlfriend. I'll have to do all that sloppy dating stuff. Now, what is it you do again?'

Adam could feel the blush reaching his ears, but

Danny was having fun. 'Oh, yeah – I have to hold her hand in the dark. What else? Nah, nah, don't tell me ... arm around the shoulders ... what's the next bit? I'm sure I remember ... That's it!' he yelled triumphantly, causing at least three people to turn and stare at them. 'Then I have to lean across and give her a great big smoochy sloppy *kiss*!'

Danny reached over and shook Adam warmly by the hand. 'Thanks for reminding me, Adam,' he said seriously. 'Listen – if you come along, I won't forget all that stuff. Maybe you'd sit behind us and, like, whisper to me what to do next ... Will you do that, Adam? Will you do that for me?'

Adam was crimson with embarrassment by this stage and had begun counting the lace-holes in his boots. 'Sorry, I don't think I –' he began.

Danny gave him an affectionate biff on the head. 'Adam – you need to chill out! Big-time! I'm only joking!'

Then he decided he'd better not torture Adam any further; it wasn't fun when it worked this well. 'Listen, Adam – I mean, we could go in the afternoon. So it's not like a date. It's just three people going to a movie. Okay?'

Adam looked up and gave a lopsided grin.

'Okay, amigo?' repeated Danny.

'Okay,' said Adam finally.

* * *

'Hi, Adam, love! Hi, Danny!' called Adam's mam as she came in from work. She managed to drop her bag in the corner, take her coat off and leave her keys on the table, all in the one movement. 'It's really getting cold these evenings. Did you have a good day?' she continued, without waiting for an answer, as she went into the kitchen and switched on the kettle. 'I hope you've done your homework, Adam. Have you?' she called.

'Yeah, it's done,' replied Adam from the couch, where he was lying watching TV. 'Mam, Danny says he'll take me to see *Alien Empire* on Saturday. Can I go?'

'Sure, whatever,' Deirdre replied, her eyes scanning the paper she had picked up.

'Great!' said Adam, making a thumbs-up sign across at Danny.

Danny went into the kitchen to talk to Adam's mother. She had sat down at the table and was having a cup of tea and a cigarette. She would take a drag of the cigarette and then, while she exhaled, pick at the skin around the fingernails of her free hand. Danny noticed that her hands were trembling.

'Hi, Danny,' she said. 'Do you want a cup?'

'Nah, I'm grand,' replied Danny. 'Deirdre, I'm a bit worried about Adam,' he went on quickly, after pausing to check that Adam was still watching television.

Deirdre sighed. 'Go on,' she said.

'He doesn't seem himself, you know? He's very jittery, and he can't take a joke or anything. I think maybe those lads in school are giving him a hard time.'

'Look, we've already been through all this with him,' said Deirdre tetchily. 'I know they're slagging him a bit, but he's just going to have to

51

toughen up. Everyone has to learn how to take a bit of teasing.'

'Well ...' replied Danny, unsure now, 'I dunno; I think maybe it's worse than that. They pelted him with milk the other day.'

'Don't I know?' Deirdre's voice went up a notch. 'Who do you think had to clean it all? It took me ages. Ah, Danny, sometimes he would do your head in. Why didn't he run a bit faster? Why couldn't he have scared them off? Even if he'd gone inside and told a teacher ...'

Deirdre took a sip of tea and began to pick at the nails on her other hand.

'Maybe he's not able, you know,' began Danny. 'It's not like him to be so ...' He searched for the right phrase, then shrugged. 'He's just so scared of everything now.'

Deirdre gazed out the window. 'He's always been a bit like that, ever since the time in the hospital when he was small.'

'When was that?'

'Oh, years ago,' said Deirdre. 'When he was

about two or three. He'd fallen off the little low wall outside and broken his arm. We brought him to the hospital, and they set the arm, but it wasn't right. So he had to go back and have an operation to put a pin in the arm. It should have been straightforward, but it wasn't. There were infections and what-have-you, and it just didn't heal. In the end it took another two weeks before it was sorted out and he could go home. His da and I took turns to stay in with him, but it was desperate.' She shook her head at the memory. 'Adam took it very hard. He'd scream and call your name when you had to go ... He'd been talking great up to then, but after that things changed. He didn't talk again for months and he got terribly clingy. He just became petrified of everything.'

'Poor little bloke,' said Danny.

Deirdre sighed and took another sip of tea. A hard look came into her eyes. 'Yeah. But I'll tell you something, Danny, I don't need this right now. I've got enough on my mind, what with your grandad in hospital in cloud-cuckoo land, Jim doing killer shifts, and hassle at work. And there's worse to come ... I may as well tell you, Danny: it looks like I'll be out of work in a couple of months. Before Christmas. Things are very tight. There'll be some changes.' She inhaled deeply and continued, 'The car will have to go back ... it's no joke.' She bit her thumbnail, and Danny saw her eyes filling up.

'Ah, sorry, Deirdre!' he said, feeling guilty now for worrying her further. 'If it helps, I'll go and visit Grandad a bit more, and I could –'

'I wouldn't wish it on you, Danny,' Deirdre interrupted. 'I hate going to that place. Oh, don't get me wrong, it's nice and clean, and the nurses are lovely. I just can't stand it when he doesn't know me. His own daughter! The other day I went to give him a kiss, and you'd think I'd tried to stab him! He nearly yelled the place down.'

If you can laugh sadly, that was what Deirdre did. 'It's terrible to see someone you love change like that – not even knowing where they are or who they are. I'll tell you something, Danny,

Adam's brilliant with him. I couldn't face it without him there. They laugh and joke like a pair of kids. Adam goes along with him.'

Danny reckoned he'd better say something positive while Deirdre's eyes were tear-free. 'Look, Deirdre, don't worry about Adam,' he said. 'I'll look out for him. Anyway, he's bound to cheer up a bit at the thought of going to the pictures on Saturday!' Danny grinned his most enthusiastic grin, though he didn't really feel like smiling. 'Adam will be grand,' he finished.

'He'll have to be,' said Deirdre, stubbing out her cigarette firmly.

* * *

It was a crisp, frosty morning, with a fine mist of water droplets over the car and on the grass. Adam took a slice of bread and stuffed it in his jacket pocket so that he'd have plenty of crumbs for the starling if it appeared. Then he waited in the hall until Mam came downstairs.

'You're keen this morning! A real early bird!' she said.

Adam said nothing, just opened the door to go outside.

'Are things a bit better for you in school now?' Mam asked, as she started up the car. 'It'll all sort itself out in the end, you'll see,' she said, before he could reply.

The starling was there! At the first set of lights, the bird watched Adam from the top of a telegraph pole. Near the footbridge, he was perched on an electricity fuse-box that had posters all over it. Then Adam lost sight of him.

He could hardly believe what he saw when they reached school. The starling was waiting – not moving, not pecking or hopping, just perched on the corner of the school building, waiting – when Adam got out of the car.

Adam was astonished. He was about to say something to his mam, but somehow he felt that if he spoke about it, the starling would go away.

He waved goodbye to Deirdre and walked slowly past the bird. As he passed, he dropped a few breadcrumbs. The starling regarded them seriously, then flew down and pecked at them in rapid movements. Adam stood completely still. The little bird was only centimetres from his feet.

'There you go, starling,' he said softly. 'I hope you like your breakfast.'

The bird hopped over to the edge of the grass, paused for a moment, then took off in the direction of the schoolyard. 'See you later, then,' said Adam, walking happily into school.

He actually enjoyed school that morning. When he came in, Niamh was sitting on his desk, talking to Conor. They were laughing at something Niamh's little sister had said the previous day. Niamh was always telling stories about her little sister Amy's antics. Half the time, Adam suspected they weren't even true, but they were fun to listen to, so no one cared.

Niamh began the tale again, for Adam: 'Adam! Guess what Amy said yesterday in the yard.'

Adam put down his bag and went over. 'What?' he asked.

'Well, one of the babies' – they all called the

57

infants 'babies' – 'had stepped on a worm, and they were all standing around looking at it. "Ah, God!" says Tommy. "I think he's dead," and they all looked sad. Jordan even began to cry. So what does Amy go and do?'

Adam and Conor shook their heads obligingly.

'She got two little leaves and put them on the ground on either side of the worm, and then she said, "It's okay, it's okay, little wormie. Now you've got wings. You can fly up to heaven and be a worm angel!"'

Niamh and Adam and Conor all burst out laughing, but just then footsteps and general shushing announced Miss Hill's arrival. A few minutes later, Conor passed Adam a piece of paper with a picture of the worm angel on it. He'd drawn a giant worm with a long robe and two huge wings, floating up through the clouds towards heaven. At the top of the page, in large letters, he'd written 'HEAVEN – ENTRANCE THIS WAY'.

By break-time the weather was sunny and clear, even though it was still fairly cold. Adam could see lots of starlings, perhaps twenty of them, in a line on the telegraph wires. There was no sign of his starling, though.

But later, as the class was lining up to go inside, the starling appeared once again. He was perched on his usual corner of the roof, his head cocked to one side, watching the children as they passed by beneath him. When Adam passed, he dropped some more crumbs, and the bird seemed to nod a thank-you before flying down to peck them up.

Suddenly Shane, who had gone back to the playground to get his jumper, came running up to the starling. He stamped his foot and yelled, 'Yah! Get out of it!' at the little bird. Startled, the starling took off almost vertically and quickly flew away.

'What did you do that for?' shouted Adam.

'What's it to you?' asked Shane, shouldering his way ahead of Adam in the line. 'Thick bird. It's just a bird, Adam. A stupid bird,' he finished.

5

THROWING STONES

Adam woke with the feeling that something good was going to happen. For a start, it was light, which meant it couldn't be a school morning. There was the sound of a radio playing downstairs, and the smell of toast. It took a few moments for him to remember that he was going to see the movie later.

Adam stretched and sat up, knocking a precariously-balanced pile of books off the end of the bed. The thud alerted Mam, who came in to see what had happened.

'Was that you falling out of bed? Maybe we should put you back in your cot!' She smiled mischievously.

Adam grinned back, delighted to see her in good form. She was wearing jeans and an old red sweatshirt, and her long hair was tied back in a ponytail. 'You look really nice, Mam,' he said. 'You do! You look like a teenager,' he insisted, as she began shaking her head.

Deirdre looked down at her old jeans and pulled at the faded top. 'You must be joking! These are my rags!' But she was smiling, and she gave him a quick hug and ruffled his hair.

'Are you coming with me to see Grandad this morning?' she asked, the smile beginning to fade from her eyes. 'He loves to see you, and –'

'Sure!' interrupted Adam. 'You don't have to make me go, Mam. I like seeing him.'

Deirdre paused on her way out the bedroom door. 'I know, love. I only meant you're very good with him and he loves to see you.' She closed the door and began going downstairs.

'But we have to be back in time for me to go to the pictures!' Adam yelled down the stairs after her. Deirdre didn't reply.

* * *

Grandad was sitting bolt upright in a chair which had a wooden table attached to it. He had his arms folded and there were some loose sheets of paper and a pen on the table in front of him. His eyes were fixed on some point towards the far end of the room. Birdy was on the other side of the ward, in his favourite chair, chirping softly. Two old ladies sat huddled together, leafing through a copy of *Woman's Own* without speaking.

Deirdre had gone to park the car, as usual, so Adam came in alone. It seemed to take her longer to park the car at each visit. Then sometimes she'd have to talk to the nurses, keeping her out of the ward for another five minutes or so.

Adam walked quietly over to his grandfather, his shoes squeaking on the lino. The sound seemed huge in the silent room. He sat in the chair beside the old man.

'Morning, Granddad.'

'Shhh! *Shhh!*' whispered Grandad urgently. 'Fold your arms. She said fold your arms, Billy. She's just gone out to talk to the master.'

Adam hastily folded his arms. He leaned over and whispered into the old man's ear, 'What are you looking at?'

Grandad hurriedly glanced at the door to see that no one was coming before he replied, 'The board. The board, Billy. We've to learn that poem up on the board by the time she gets back!' He began murmuring:

'Under a spreading chestnut tree
The village smithy stands ...'

Adam followed his gaze. There was a blank wall, flanked on either side by wheelchairs; a small table, with a vase of wilting flowers perched off-centre on it; and a big gilt-framed picture showing a farmyard scene. No blackboard.

So we're in school, thought Adam. *And I'm Billy.* 'Hey, Grand – I mean Joe.' Adam nudged Grandad's elbow. 'What age are we?'

'What kind of a question is that, you eejit! We're nine! We'll be in with the master and the big boys next year. Oh, I hope she's not telling him about us!'

'Telling him what?'

Grandad nodded in the direction of the window. 'About the yard. About throwing stones in the yard.'

Suddenly Adam remembered an old story that his grandad had told him, before he'd become ill. It was Grandad's most famous school story – the one where he'd been caned. He had been caught throwing stones in the yard, so the story went, and had been sent to the master and beaten. But Grandad had always maintained that he and his friend hadn't been throwing stones, they'd been *pitching* them – little gentle throws, designed to land in a specific spot. Billy must have been the friend who had got in trouble with him. Adam thought he remembered that Grandad had actually gone straight home after the beating, he'd been so upset. When he'd arrived home and told his mother the sorry tale, she had marched him right back to the master for another beating! *Tough days,* thought Adam.

Then he had an idea. 'But we weren't throwing

stones, Gr – Joe!' he said reassuringly. 'The mistress knows that.'

'We weren't?' quavered the old man, with watery eyes.

'Nah, of course not. We were collecting them. Yeah, that's right. There was a big pothole in the tarmac ...'

'What are you talking about, Billy?' demanded Grandad, his expression anxious.

I'd better get this right, thought Adam. 'Miss – the teacher asked you and me to collect those stones at break-time. That's right. She said there was a hole in the ground and one of the little ones might fall into it. So she asked you and me to collect enough stones to fill the hole.' He paused for effect. 'And then we were to pitch the stones into the hole.' He hoped the word 'pitch' would ring a bell. He waited, smiling and nodding in an effort to convince Grandad.

The old man began to look more hopeful. 'Is that right?'

'That's right,' said Adam firmly. 'And now she's

telling the master how great we are.'

'No!' Grandad's voice was trembling.

'Yep!' said Adam. 'She's telling him that we helped her and we should get a reward.' He was worried he'd gone too far. Did they get rewards in those days?

But he needn't have worried. The old man relaxed and, at last, unfolded his arms. 'Do you know what, Billy?' he said, turning to Adam. 'I think you're right. That must be what she's doing.'

By the time Deirdre came in, Grandad had dozed off, resting against his 'school desk'.

'Don't wake him, Mam,' said Adam. 'He's had a tough day at school.'

6

THE RUBBISH BIN

When they got home, Deirdre went straight into the kitchen and made herself a cup of tea before tackling a pile of ironing. Adam came into the room as she was doing it. 'Mam? It's nearly half-twelve. Are you bringing me up or is Dad?'

'Up where? Where is it you're going?' she asked, unplugging the iron wearily and setting it down on the worktop.

'Remember, Mam? *Alien Empire!* Two o'clock!' asked Adam, not believing she could have forgotten something so important. 'I said I'd meet Danny up there at about a quarter to two.'

'Ah, heck!' said Deirdre, remembering

something. 'I'm supposed to be meeting Joan at around one.' Adam looked stricken. 'Don't worry. Don't start whining ...' She tightened her ponytail and began biting her nail as she thought what to do.

'I'll tell you what. I'll leave you up there early and you can hang around, look at the shops, whatever, until your picture starts. Okay?'

'Okay,' replied Adam. He was disappointed, though. He had been hoping that she'd go up to the shops with him and they could have a chat before the film began. *Why is she always so busy? Why does Dad have to work shifts?* He felt the sadness and self-pity rising up in him and had to swallow back a lump in his throat.

Deirdre saw the glitter of tears in his eyes.

'Ah, Adam! Grow up! Don't be such a baby!' she snapped. 'What's the matter? You're going to the pictures, you've no school. I don't understand you at all.'

Her voice softened a little when she saw his face, red now, and she took a tissue and rubbed away the tears. 'Here,' she said, reaching into her bag and opening her purse. She handed him a five-pound note. 'You spent your own money on your grandad the other day. You're a good lad. Spend that on yourself before you go in.'

Adam folded the note carefully and put it in his pocket. 'Thanks, Mam,' he said.

* * *

At one o'clock, Deirdre left Adam at the round-about beside the shopping centre. 'Now, make sure you buy yourself something to eat, Adam. Something decent, not sweets. Right?' She opened her purse and took out another five-pound note. 'Enjoy yourself, love.'

Adam took the money and got out of the car. 'Thanks, Mam. See you later.'

He waved as she drove off. As he did, he noticed a group of boys about his age hanging around at the bus stop across the road. He felt suddenly self-conscious about waving; he quickly lowered his arm and walked up to the car park.

He was planning to go into the shopping centre and get something to eat in McDonald's, but the queues were snaking almost out the door and there were no free tables. He walked on round the car park instead, and sat on a bench near the taxi rank. The taxi drivers were sitting in their cars, some listening to the radio, some reading papers propped up on their steering-wheels. Then someone would get a taxi from the front of the rank, and they'd all start their engines and drive two or three feet forward before settling down to read again.

Adam pulled a half-eaten bar of chocolate out of his pocket, rubbed the fluff off it, and started to eat. From where he sat, he could see down to the main road and the park opposite the shopping centre. His gaze travelled on, to where the land seemed to melt into the sky, with an almost-imperceptible line of white separating the two strips of grey.

To the right of his view, the land sloped gradually upwards to form low hills and, in the distance, the Dublin mountains. His school lay in that direction, almost the last man-made structure between the city and the hills.

Far in the distance, he could see a flock of birds wheeling and diving. *They must be seagulls,* he thought. *That means it's going to rain.* Miss Hill had told them that. 'If there are seagulls far inland, the rain's not far behind,' she'd said. 'They all fly inland to get shelter, so the rain must be on its way in from the coast.' Adam liked it when Miss Hill told them about nature, or when she told them old sayings like 'Red sky at night, shepherd's delight.' She'd grown up on a farm, and sometimes told them funny stories about things she'd done as a child.

He liked Miss Hill, but even so, he couldn't imagine her being able to help him out with Rory and Shane and PJ. He'd thought about telling her, especially about the milk; but he'd felt she might make it worse – get their parents in, and his mam, and set up meetings with the principal ... He sighed and threw the chocolate wrapper towards the bin. *Better just carry on and hope they'll stop.*

He got up and picked up the wrapper, which had bounced off the side of the bin and fallen on the ground. Suddenly he saw a flock of starlings wheeling in from the left, heading towards the back of the shopping centre. There was a parking lot there, for lorries delivering goods, and it was full of bins and skips holding all the rubbish from the shops. *They'll probably find plenty of food there,* Adam thought, and decided to go round and see.

As he turned the corner, he heard voices. The starlings had landed on the ground near one of the big wheelie bins and had begun pecking at the half-eaten chips and lumps of bread that littered the ground, but a sudden bang made them all take off. Adam looked around to see what had caused it.

There were four kids behind one of the skips – well, three kids, maybe Danny's age, and a bigger boy. They were lighting pieces of paper and throwing them into the skip. With a sinking heart, Adam recognised the jackets the boys were wearing. Didn't he see them every day at school? It was PJ, Rory and Shane. The teenager was probably PJ's big brother, Niall, the one he was always boasting about.

Perhaps if Adam had run then, he could have got away. But he'd been spotted. 'If it isn't the school sap!' said PJ, nudging the bigger boy. Rory and Shane turned and started towards Adam.

'Nah, he's not a sap,' said Rory. 'He's just a dope.'

Adam began slowly backing away, but Niall moved quickly as a snake and grabbed him by the arm. 'Who's this?' he asked PJ.

'No one,' said PJ scornfully.

'Just Adam. Little Addy-waddam,' sneered Shane. Niall pinned Adam's arm behind his back and held him tight.

Up close, Niall was not a pretty sight. He had bleached hair with greasy black roots, and one of his pale eyebrows was pierced with a grubby silver ring, which wobbled when he spoke or moved. His skin was covered in red and purple pimples, which had taken over his whole chin area like an invading army. Underneath these, the skin itself was an unhealthy-looking shade of greenish-white. Niall was gripping Adam so tightly that Adam could smell his breath. It smelled of drink.

'Well, Adam,' drawled Niall, like some demented talk-show host, 'what a lovely shiny jacket you have on. I'd say that cost your mammy a lotta money, hmm? Rich boy, are you?'

Adam didn't answer. He knew nothing he said would make any difference.

'Is he?' Niall asked the others, who stood sniggering and watching in a huddle like grubby little vultures.

'Is he what?' said Shane, whose mouth was hanging open.

'Is he a *rich kid*, you dopes?' yelled Niall.

They nodded vigorously.

'Yeah, his mammy and daddy give him everything – only kid,' said Rory, as if that explained everything.

It certainly seemed good enough for Niall, who

shook his head. 'Tsk, tsk, Adam. Very greedy. You're meant to share, you know. Don't they teach you that in school?'

Adam's heart was pounding so hard he could feel it in his throat. He thought he might be about to throw up.

Suddenly Niall gave him a hard jab in the stomach with his free hand. Adam doubled over, trying to get his breath. The others rushed over, eager to join in now that the first blow had been struck.

'Leave him alone!' roared Niall.

'What?' said PJ in disbelief.

'You eejit, you're all in school with him. You can't beat him up, you'll get caught. Here, hold him for me.'

Like trained dogs, they obeyed quickly, pinning Adam's arms behind his back in vice-like grips. Niall rapidly went through Adam's pockets and found the two fivers his mam had given him. He thrust them into the back pocket of his own jeans.

'Oh, dear! Poor Adam,' continued Niall, patting Adam down and tenderly zipping up his jacket.

'You can't help getting into trouble, can you? What were you looking for?'

Adam had no idea what he was talking about. He stared at Niall, ashen-faced. What was he going to do next?

They were standing beside one of the big wheelie bins; the roll-top lid was open and there were a few bin-bags lying on the bottom. Niall continued, 'Yeah, you were looking in the bin for the money you'd lost – you should be more careful Adam – and guess what happened? Here's the fun part! You just fell in!'

Finally, Adam realised what was going to happen. He felt a surge of heat and panic begin to well up from deep inside him. To his shame, tears began to prick behind his eyelids.

'Here – let me help you!' said Niall, in the same sinister, kind voice. He gave Adam a leg up and then, in one rapid movement, heaved him head-first into the filthy, stinking bin. The others stared in disbelief as Niall rolled the lid down and held the two handles together.

'For God's sake!' he bawled at the three of them. 'Go and get a plank or something to jam this with, you thicks!' His knuckles whitened with the effort of keeping the iron handles pressed together. 'Or do you want us all to get caught?'

Quickly, Rory picked up a broken sweeping-brush and thrust it into Niall's hand. With a bang, Niall rammed it through the handles, then checked to see that it would hold. It did. He turned and gave the bin a final kick. 'Now, you three, leg it home or you're for it!'

'What about the money?' asked PJ.

'What money?' sneered Niall. 'I don't have any money. Now beat it!' he roared.

Having seen what had happened to Adam, the three boys didn't need to be told again. They ran.

Inside the bin, Adam lay on his side, with his knees pulled up to his chest and his hands clasped around them to stop himself shaking. *Please don't let Niall come back for me,* he prayed over and over, as he heard the sound of the boys' feet disappearing into the distance. For a few minutes he lay perfectly still, too petrified to move in case Niall was still there. His stomach was aching where Niall had punched him. His teeth were clenched, and when he tried to unclench them he found they wouldn't stop chattering.

He bit his lip. Then he gave up the struggle and let the tears flow freely. Soon he was crying in great gulping sobs, his whole body shaking.

The stench inside the bin was disgusting, and as the shock and terror waned, Adam began to recognise the individual foul smells. Banana, he could smell banana – and crisps, and sour milk and rotten meat and wet cardboard and black plastic bags ... and rotten apples ... and chips and lumps and clumps of black filth coating the inside of the bin ...

'Let me out!' Adam sat up and began banging against the lid. But his cry had been more of a whisper. He tried again. 'Let me out! Help!' his mind screamed. But the words didn't reach his mouth. Adam could feel them, like sharp, black stones lodged in his throat.

He fell back against the side of the bin and put his head in his hands. What if he was left there all night? They hardly ever emptied these bins. What if a week went by? What if Niall came back and threw in a match?

He'd lost all track of time. Maybe his mam was home already, worrying, wondering where he was. Suddenly he thought of Danny, waiting for him. The thought of everyone looking for him panicked Adam even more. He retched, and the smell of sick was added to the stench in the bin.

For a long time Adam sat huddled with his back against the side of the bin, his arms hugging his knees and his head buried in his arms. He had stopped crying.

Tick ... tick ... tick ...

What was that? Adam's head jerked up and he tried to see if the noise was coming from inside or outside the bin. He peered through the gloom. Then he heard it again, faster: *tick-tick, tick-tick, tick-tick.* It was over his head, on the roof of his filthy metal prison. It was ... it sounded like ... a bird, sort of running along the roof of the bin. Then it would stop and peck. The sound was amazingly loud from where Adam sat. An image of a bird wearing metal boots came into his mind – his starling in little bird boots with steel tips! *I must be losing it,* thought Adam, almost crying with laughter at the picture.

The laughter helped. A new calm came over Adam, and he found he was brave enough to shuffle over on his knees to the tiny crack of white where daylight came through between the bin and the lid.

'Starling?' he said softly. 'Starling, is it you?' He thought he could hear the bird directly over his head. 'Starling?'

He could just see a tiny black triangle, then another, breaking the line. The bird was obviously perched on the rim of the bin, with the claws of one foot curled around it.

Adam took a deep breath, filling his lungs with the foul air in the bin. 'Help!' he yelled, at last finding his voice. '*Help me!*' he roared, banging at the bin with his fists. Then he sat back and began kicking the sides of the bin with his boots, over and over.

It still stank, and it was still pitch-dark except for a tiny crack of light, but Adam's fear was gone. He was raging. He banged and yelled and stamped, and all the while he felt the anger like a swirling, bubbling, flowing river inside him. Rage

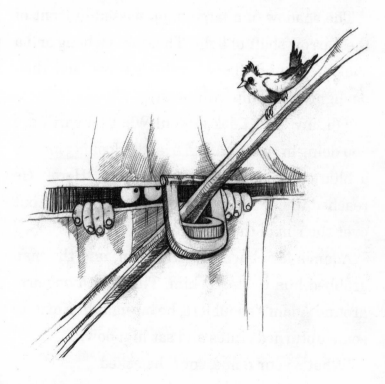

for the punch in his stomach, for the filth in the bin, for his imprisonment, for the jeering and the insults and the shoves and the jibes. A lifetime of rage.

'Okay, okay. Hold on. Steady on!' A deep voice carried over the noises in the bin and the anger in his head. 'You'll be out of there in as a second, whoever you are. Calm down!'

The shadow of a large hand passed in front of the narrow shaft of light. There was a bang and a shake, a sound like a crashing wave, and then daylight, air. White, white air.

'Oh, my God! Look at you! What on earth are you doing in there?' A big, friendly-looking man in a blue shirt stood staring at him – 'Here!' He reached under Adam's arms and hauled him out over the rim of the wheelie bin.

Adam's legs buckled with relief, and the man grabbed him to steady him. Then, with one arm around Adam's shoulders, he brought him over to some upturned crates and sat him down.

'What's your name, son?' he asked.

'Adam,' replied Adam, still shaking.

The man squeezed Adam's shoulder reassuringly. 'Okay, Adam. You're all right now. I'm Les. Now, how the hell did you end up in the bin?' He carried on without waiting for an answer. 'You could have been stuck there for days. Hardly anyone uses these bins – they use the other ones at the front. God – you could have died in there!' He shook his head in disbelief. 'And you're only, what, eight?'

'N-nine,' said Adam.

'Well, whoever did that to you deserves a good hiding, a good kick in the ...' He stopped. 'Do you know the guy who did it?'

Adam paused, then shook his head. 'Some big guy. He took my m-money and shoved me in there.'

'God, they should all be strung up.' The man looked closely at Adam. 'Did he beat you up?' Adam shook his head again. 'Well, that's something. Come on inside and we'll clean you up.'

7

LINDA'S PLAN

Les brought Adam up a flight of black metal stairs and into the back of the dry-cleaners where he worked. Adam stood quietly, while they all fussed over him, and waited for his hands to stop shaking.

A middle-aged woman came running over and took his jacket. 'The poor child!' she exclaimed, giving Adam a little pat before quickly cleaning the filthy coat with a kind of hot spray-gun. Another girl gave him a damp cloth and helped him clean up his jeans. Les showed him where the cloakroom was, and Adam went in to wash his face and hands.

For a few moments, with his hands deep in warm soapy water, Adam closed his eyes and leaned his head against the mirror in front of him. The water was almost too hot, and Adam felt his hands tingle and throb as the blood warmed up. He sighed. He'd always loved the smell of the drycleaners. Now it was as if he was surrounded by heat and steam. He could hear the hiss of the large cleaning-machines working away outside the cloakroom door. The sound and the warmth calmed him. He still felt sore and bruised, but at least the panic had subsided. And he was clean.

Suddenly he remembered the film. What about Danny and Linda? He looked at his watch in disbelief. It said five to two! Adam shook it and held it up to his ear. It was still ticking, but Adam found it difficult to believe that so little time had passed. It felt as if days had passed since his mam had dropped him off.

He knew that if he moved quickly he'd actually make it to the cinema by two o'clock. Then no one would have to know. He didn't want sympathy, or questions, or all the sentences that start with 'You know what you should do ...'

And anyway, there was something else – something small and steely growing inside him. A feeling like a smooth, hard marble, polished and glinting. Anger.

'I've got to go,' he said to Les as he came out of the tiny cloakroom.

Les looked surprised. 'Do you not want me to bring you home?' he asked, jangling car keys ready in his hand. 'Where are you going? Have you money?'

Adam nodded. 'I'm meeting my cousin,' he said. 'I'll be fine. Thanks for everything.' He headed towards the door of the shop.

'Okay, okay!' laughed Les. 'You're quick to perk up! Come back to me here if you need a lift or if you see that fella again. Here's a fiver.'

'Ah, no, I couldn't ...' began Adam, but Les folded the fiver up into a tiny square and pressed it into his hand.

'Go on with you. Take it.'

Adam took the note shyly. 'Thanks. I – I ...' He trailed off.

'It's nothing. Go on!' smiled Les, tousling his hair. 'And try to keep out of trouble, you hear?'

'I will. Thanks, Les; thanks, eh ... everyone.' Adam smiled and closed the door.

He raced up to the cinemas, nimbly darting in and out between shoppers. It was just a minute after two. Danny and Linda were sitting on the stairs near the ice-cream shop. Lines of people were moving into various cinemas, handing over their tickets and disappearing into the blackness.

'Adam! Where were you?' called Danny, jumping to his feet and nudging Linda. She stood up too and smiled at Adam.

'Hiya, Adam. How are ya?' she asked, handing him his ticket. 'Come on, they've all gone in. I'd say the trailers have started.'

Adam took his ticket and murmured a handful of apologies. They sat down in the cinema just as the opening credits began to roll.

Later, in McDonald's, Adam tried to give Danny

Les's fiver for the fries and Cokes he'd bought for the three of them. Danny wouldn't hear of it, and Adam felt strangely guilty putting the money back in his pocket.

'You hang on to it,' said Danny. 'Sure we're loaded, aren't we, Linda? We get paid a fortune working in our place!'

Linda nodded. 'Get yourself sweets or something for school,' she said.

At the mention of school, Adam felt a quick hiccup of fear, as if he'd been prodded in the stomach. A sudden surge of panic went through him.

Danny must have seen something in his expression, because he glanced at Linda and his eyes seemed to ask her a question.

'Is school tough going?' she asked.

Adam could see where the conversation was leading. He shrugged as if he could actually shake the topic off, the way a dog shakes off cold water.

'Look, Adam,' interrupted Danny, 'you don't need to pretend. Why don't you let me sort those fellas out? I could talk to them for you.'

Adam tried to imagine Danny dealing with Shane, Rory and PJ. He had a mental picture of them barking and nipping at Danny like dirty little terrier puppies. It would be easy for Danny – one swift kick and they'd be off, howling.

That's what I have to do. The thought hit Adam with a heavy thud of realisation. *I have to make them stop. And it has to be soon, before it gets worse* ... The thought of something worse than being locked in a wheelie bin made Adam shudder.

'Well?' said Linda. He hadn't realised she was speaking to him. 'Adam?' she asked. 'Isn't that right? You have to stand up to bullies?'

Adam just nodded.

'How many are there?' she continued.

'Three,' said Adam.

'Right – there'll be a ringleader, then, and the others will be gofers,' said Linda. Adam looked confused. 'You know, go-fors – they get bossed around, fetch and carry for the ringleader,' she explained.

Adam nodded again. That was Rory, Shane and

PJ exactly: Rory bossed, and the others sniggered and helped.

'Always listen to Linda,' said Danny, as if he were reciting one of the Ten Commandments. 'Women – they're all very good on the old psychology. And Linda's the best of all.' He tapped his head and looked thoughtful.

'Shut up, you!' laughed Linda, giving him a thump on the arm. 'Adam' – she leaned over to make her point more forcefully – 'you know I'm right. You have to do something ... and you *can*, too. Find the ringleader and just stand up for yourself. You'll probably only have to do it once.' She sat back.

'Good thinking, Batgirl!' laughed Danny. 'You tell him!' He took a noisy slurp of his Coke. 'She's absotively, posilutely correct!' He let out a loud belch .

Linda gave Danny the eye, but he pretended not to see. 'Come on, amigo. You're better than they are. Find the leader, face him down. Adam rules, bullies drool – eh, drools!'

8

ADAM'S SECRET

It was Monday morning, and Adam had a plan.

He'd got up early and had some breakfast with his dad when he heard him come in from work. It was still pitch-dark outside, and they'd spent over half an hour chatting and drinking mugs of tea in the warm kitchen.

'I know things are hard for you at school right now, Adam,' Dad had said. 'And if you like, I'll go in and talk to the teacher. But sometimes it's better to sort things on your own.'

Adam nodded.

'After all, the teacher won't be there all the time.'

Again, Adam nodded. 'I know, Da. It's fine – it will be fine. And I know she won't be around all the time.' He thought of the bin behind the shopping centre. No teacher there. And the strange thing was that Adam felt Miss Hill wouldn't have fared much better than he had – not with Niall. 'It's okay, Dad. I'll sort it on my own.'

And that, more or less, was the plan.

* * *

There was a substitute teacher in fourth class; Miss Hill was sick and wouldn't be in for a few days. The sub was new, and very young. She looked like a student teacher. By the time Adam came into school, there was already an excited, dangerous atmosphere in the classroom. All the children were changing places to sit beside their friends, pretending that they always sat there. Rory was beside PJ, with Shane in the desk behind. Miss Hill never let them sit together, even for watching videos. She had more sense.

Adam's usual place was empty, and Niamh was

at her desk, beside his. When Adam walked in, Rory, Shane and PJ looked quickly at one another, as if wondering what was going to happen. They stole shifty little glances at each other and at Adam – except for PJ, who couldn't even look at him, but started sharpening his pencil vigorously. Adam deliberately kept his face blank and looked right back at them. He hoped the look said something like 'Things are different now' or 'No more Mr Nice Guy'. Anything apart from 'Wimp who gets shoved into bins'.

Adam said hi to Niamh and sat down, glancing at PJ's desk again. Shane and PJ looked decidedly scared; they were glancing nervously at Adam, then back at Rory. Even Rory looked slightly rattled, not knowing what to expect.

Adam turned back towards Niamh and began talking. He felt a tiny thrill of power. They were scared that Adam was going to tell, that he already had told. For the first time, they were scared of him. *Let them sweat for a while,* he thought.

The substitute teacher was sitting at Miss Hill's

desk, looking through textbooks and a timetable, obviously planning the day. She didn't seem to notice the noise in the room – kids swapping stories, swinging on chairs, banging rulers, yelling and laughing. She was small and young, with a pointy, timid-looking face.

The noise became louder and louder. Still the teacher read and shuffled pages. Kids began to get out of their places and walk around the class; she didn't even look up.

A voice rose from the back of the class: 'Miss! Hey, Miss! What are we going to do today?'

Another, louder voice, rising shrilly over all the noise: 'Yeah! Where's Miss Hill?'

No reply.

'Hey, Missus!' Colm's voice. Colm was always trying to get a laugh. The only problem was that he wasn't very funny, just loud. Now he bellowed, 'Missus, are you deaf?'

The young teacher shoved her chair back against the wall, so hard that it sounded like the crack of a whip. She got up, turned to the blackboard and rapidly scrawled her name in large letters: Miss Clarke. She underlined it with such force that the chalk broke and fell to the floor in three little pieces. Before a titter could break out, she whirled around, banged the hard side of the duster on the board with a loud rap, and shouted in a surprisingly deep voice: 'Right! My name is Miss Clarke. Not Teacher, Miss or' – she shuddered theatrically – 'Missus.'

She slammed the duster back onto the ledge. 'And let's get one thing straight. I am a Fully Qualified Teacher.' She sounded like an FBI agent announcing himself, complete with badge and gun. 'A fully qualified national-school teacher. I may look young. I may even still look like' – her voice was scornful – 'a *student* teacher. But I'm not.'

There wasn't a sound; everyone sat rigidly in their places. For someone so small, she had a very loud voice. She marched down the centre of the room like a tiny sergeant-major, turned and yelled again, 'I may be teaching you for some time. So get this into your heads once and for all: I am a fully qualified national school teacher! *Not* a student!' She gazed off into the distance, hands on hips, feet (in tiny black boots) firmly planted. 'And I'm damned good! You have ten seconds to sit in your proper places. Now *move it*!'

For a split second, nobody moved. Then, in a panic, the kids who had switched desks hastily gathered their belongings and scurried back to their rightful places. They kept their eyes on the floor.

By the time Miss Clarke had reached her desk again, there was total silence. All eyes were on her. She bent smoothly to retrieve the chalk, flashed a dazzling smile and said in the warm tones of an airline stewardess: 'Good morning, boys and girls. My name is Miss Clarke and I'll be with you for the next few days.'

Adam, and probably the rest of the class, wondered if they'd imagined the previous minute.

'I look forward to spending some pleasant days with you, boys and girls. Now, let's begin.'

Adam shook his head in admiration. *So that's how you do it!* he thought.

Outside, at break, fourth-class kids wasted no time telling awestruck smaller children about Miss Clarke – how she'd broken a ruler in half banging it on the table, how she'd forbidden them to talk or even to breathe loudly, how she was going to give them triple homework and detention on Friday ...

Niamh and Adam stood leaning against the only tree in the playground, in companionable silence. Conor came over. He had a packet of Chewits, and he offered them round.

'What d'ya think of your woman, then?' he asked, unwrapping another sweet and putting it in his mouth.

Adam shrugged.

'I think she's great,' said Niamh. 'Sure, she's strict, but I'd say she's nice underneath. I mean, she has to be tough – you know what some of them are like.'

Conor smiled. 'Wasn't it gas when she picked up

97

Rory's book and held it like it was radioactive?' He mimicked her mousy expression and piercing voice: '"Am I supposed to *correct* this? Do you *really* expect me to spend my valuable time searching these grubby half-sentences for your answers? Blunt pencil! No margin! No capital letters!"'

Adam laughed. 'And when she let go of the copy and wiped her fingers with a tissue ...'

'Yeah! Well, you would too – it's filthy!' exclaimed Niamh.

'He won't be taking her on today,' said Conor. 'He looked really scared, didn't he?'

Niamh nodded. 'So did Shane. I think maybe they're in trouble for something else. They both look pretty worried.'

Adam bit his lip. Here was a chance to tell his friends what had happened. He'd told nobody, not even his mam. He'd locked it away in the small, dark box of his mind. But it hadn't gone away. Rolling around inside him was the marble of anger – steely and hard, and very much there. He said nothing.

A small movement on the playground wall caught his eye. His starling! Sidestepping along, then pausing and looking around – it was like a little dance to some inaudible bird rhythm. Look up, wait, look across, wait, look down, wait …

The bird looked over at Adam, and Adam had to fight the impulse to wave and say 'Hi.' Instead, he smiled.

'Hello? Ground control to Adam … come in, please!' Niamh laughed as she waved her hands in front of Adam's face.

'Sorry.' Adam shook his head. 'I was just looking at the starling.'

'Where?' asked Conor and Niamh together. Adam pointed, but there was nothing on the wall any more.

'You're daft, Adam,' said Niamh fondly.

'You sure are!' agreed Conor.

Adam smiled as the bell rang and they headed back across the playground. He remembered the bird footsteps – or, rather, claw-steps – on the roof of the wheelie bin. Could it be? *Maybe he follows me, maybe he looks out for me,* Adam thought wonderingly.

Back in class, there wasn't a sound from anyone. Adam sat at his desk by the window, answering geography questions. Miss Clarke paced up and down, silently stopping every now and then behind some unfortunate person who'd made a mistake, prodding her bony little finger at the error and sighing in irritation. Adam thought of Grandad's schooldays. Miss Clarke would have fitted in well there.

Then Adam looked up, feeling he was being watched, and saw the starling actually on the ledge outside his window, stepping back and forth on his impossibly thin legs. Adam could see every feather – the brownish-green ones on his face, the fluffier, speckled ones on his breast, the long, strong tail-feathers and wing-feathers. And his eyes ... up close they still looked inky-black, but with the most delicate surround of grey ...

'You!' Adam jumped as Miss Clarke shrieked and pointed at him. 'Aaron, or – what is it?'

'Adam,' murmured Adam.

'Well, Adam, stop staring out the window! Get on with your work. You can go bird-watching outside school hours.'

There was a general smirk at Miss Clarke's humour, and Adam quickly buried his head in his book. The little bird flew off.

* * *

When school was let out, Adam waited behind for

a couple of minutes, in the hope that Rory and Shane and PJ would leave quickly and not wait for him. Miss Clarke asked him to check that all the windows were closed. Quickly, Adam opened the one beside his desk and put the remains of one of his sandwiches out on the window-ledge for the starling. Then he closed the window and gathered up his stuff.

'Bye, Miss Clarke,' he called.

'Bye, Aaron,' she replied, not looking up from her desk.

As Adam came out of the school building, some-one grabbed his elbow and called, 'Gotcha!'

Adam whirled around, his fingernails already digging into his palms, steeling himself. 'Get off!'

He stopped suddenly, seeing Niamh's friendly face – only it wasn't friendly; she looked worried. 'Oh, Adam, I'm sorry! Are you okay?' She held onto the arm she'd just grabbed and looked closely at him. 'You're really pale. Sorry for scaring you.'

'It's okay,' said Adam. 'It's just that – I thought you were someone else.'

'Nah, I saw those three running off five minutes ago. They couldn't get out of here fast enough.'

Adam smiled: the lads still didn't know if he'd told or not. It was kind of nice to think of them being scared and worried, for a change.

'Hey, Niamh?' he asked suddenly, as they walked along together. 'Did you ever hear of a bird following you?'

'Is this a joke or something?' asked Niamh.

'No, no – for real.'

'Well, I've heard of stray dogs following people, or maybe cats. But never a bird. Why?'

'Don't laugh!' said Adam, glancing at her face; she was already smiling. She had a gap between her front teeth, which made her smile even more noticeable, and mischievous green eyes. He looked down and sighed.

'Go on, Adam!' Niamh said, exasperated. 'I'm not laughing. I can't help smiling, but I'm not laughing.'

'Okay,' he went on. 'Okay – well, this sounds weird, but there's a bird that follows me. I've seen it at school, on the way to school, at the shops, in the yard ...' He stopped, checking Niamh's reaction.

'What kind of bird?' she asked, eyebrows raised but not smiling now.

'A starling,' he replied quickly. 'A small starling. Kind of scruffy.'

'And it follows you?' asked Niamh, beginning to slow down. 'Like to your house?'

Adam hesitated, then nodded.

'And then to school? Does it come inside?' She grinned and began to giggle. 'Does it follow you everywhere? Like into the bathroom?'

Adam stopped and sighed. 'No, not into the bathroom. I knew you wouldn't believe me. I told you you'd laugh.'

Then he thought of something: he'd never actually seen the starling at home. And maybe the one on the way to school was a different one – maybe it was a different one each time – maybe the one at school was just some greedy bird ...

'Forget it,' he said.

'Adam!' said Niamh, as they reached her bus stop. 'Sorry for laughing. Show me your bird tomorrow in school.'

'Yeah, right,' said Adam, sighing. 'Forget it.'

9

TROUBLE

Rain poured down outside and a strong wind whirled around the school, dashing the rain against the windowpanes. Adam watched the raindrops rolling down the smooth glass. He chose one raindrop, high up, and followed its progress all the way down. It didn't roll smoothly; it would lose speed and travel sideways, or pause, until it drifted into another bead of water; then it would be heavy enough to roll a little further. He was glad he'd chosen that particular drop to follow, though. Some drops were too tiny even to enter the race. They just landed on the windowpane and stayed there. His little drop meandered along its own route, stopping and starting, until finally it reached the rain-drenched windowsill. All the while, heavier drops lashed and splashed their more direct routes down.

There was a knock at the classroom door. Adam jumped.

'Come in!' called Miss Clarke in her shrill voice.

'Um, excuse me, Miss Hi – I mean Teacher,' said a sixth-class boy, Ronan.

'What is it? And my name is not "Teacher", it's Miss Clarke.'

Ronan tried again. 'Sorry, Miss Clarke. Shane and Rory Brennan are wanted in the principal's office. And PJ Murtagh, too.'

'Now?' enquired Miss Clarke, already fixing the three boys with her narrow-eyed gaze.

'Um, now,' replied Ronan.

Rory was already up out of his place, glancing shiftily at Shane and PJ. They filed past across the silent classroom. Rory gave a sly hiss on his way past Adam's desk: 'You're dead.' Adam felt his stomach lurch.

They were gone for ages. Miss Clarke had just

told the class to get out their lunches when the three boys returned. PJ came in first, red-eyed and hangdog; he muttered, 'Sorry, Miss,' and shuffled to his place. Shane appeared next, bottom lip quivering, head down. Finally Rory came in, surly and furious, elbowing the door closed behind him and striding over to his desk. Even Miss Clarke decided not to tackle him in that humour.

At break, Conor – who always knew everything that was going on – told Adam. Rory and Shane and PJ had been seen down at the back of the shopping centre, on Saturday setting fire to rubbish and throwing it into a skip. There'd been a small fire there later and the guards had been called. Someone had told the gardaí which school the boys were from, and the school had been contacted. The principal had hauled the boys over the coals for forty minutes, phoned their parents, and put them on report for two weeks.

Adam's first reaction was relief – if you were on report, you had to stand outside the principal's office at break-time and before school, and you had a report card to be signed daily at home and at school. You were also automatically in detention on Fridays. At least for a while he'd have a bit more peace and quiet at break-time.

Niamh ran over to Adam and Conor. 'So?' she said, gasping for breath. 'Where's your pet bird, your magpie or whatever?' She gave Adam a playful elbow in the ribs.

Adam sighed and scanned the playground. There was no sign of the starling. 'I dunno. Maybe I imagined it,' he muttered. 'I'm just going in to get my jacket. Back in a minute, lads.'

He ran up to the back door of the school. One part of him was convinced that he'd been fooling himself all along about the bird; the other part of him was planning to leave some more crumbs on his windowsill, just in case, while no one was in the classroom.

The classroom always looked like a shambles when they weren't in it – half-eaten lunches still on the desks, chairs pushed out at awkward angles, pencils and markers on the floor; even the teacher's desk looked abandoned, with open textbooks and uncapped pens. Adam quickly crumbled up a few crisps, opened his window and placed them on the sill outside.

Just as he was closing the window, he heard footsteps. Quickly, thinking it was a teacher, he knelt on the floor beside his desk and pretended to be looking for something in his schoolbag.

He didn't look up as the footsteps approached. Suddenly – *wham!* – the desk was sent slamming into the side of his face, whacking against his left ear. Adam's hands flew up to hold his throbbing face, and he whirled around.

Rory stood there, white-faced with rage, his pinched features and thin lips making him look far older than ten. 'You are so dead, you little ...' He aimed another kick at the desk, sending Adam's books and pens crashing to the floor. Adam had stood up and was edging back towards the door of the adjoining classroom.

'I knew you'd tell, you little sneak.'

'I – I –' began Adam.

'I – I – I –' mimicked Rory. 'Told on us, yeah, and we didn't even take your money. We weren't the ones that put you in there. It was Niall.' Rory was livid. 'Too scared to rat on *him*, though,' he sneered, his lips drawn back over ratty little teeth.

'I didn't tell!' stammered Adam. Why was he defending himself? This wasn't the plan!

Rory followed Adam as he backed up towards the door. 'Nah – you thought you'd be really clever – not tell about the wheelie bin. Then we wouldn't know it was you.'

'But it really wasn't me! And anyway, you ...' Adam began to find a tiny shred of courage. 'Anyway, you –'

Suddenly the bell rang, and the two of them were jerked back into the reality of the classroom. Rory was the first to react.

'Yeah, well, I should have got you when I had the chance, you sneak. And I will. You are dead!' He jabbed Adam's chest with his finger in time with the words. 'You' – jab – 'are' – jab – '*dead!*' Hard jab. Then he turned and walked out.

Adam went back to his desk, picked his stuff up off the floor, and sat down with his head in his hands. He was furious with himself and his ear hurt terribly. *So much for the plan.*

He didn't even notice the starling pecking the crumbs off the windowsill, right beside him.

* * *

Adam sat beside Grandad in the day ward, enjoying the warm stillness of the room. His ear still throbbed and pulsed, but the worst of the pain had faded. They were leafing through the evening paper together, Grandad's large fingers tracing the print in a slow, smudging trawl across the crackly pages.

When they reached an article about Elvis, the old man suddenly became animated.

'The King!' he cried, pointing at the familiar rock star in his white sequined suit.

'Oh, yeah?' said Adam, leaning across for a better view.

'He's great, he is. He's been in loads of films. We've seen them all, your mam and me.'

Adam nodded. *So today I must be Gary again.*

'Maybe there's another one coming out soon. Or maybe he's coming over to do a concert ... Let's see ...' Grandad began reading aloud in a hesitant voice:

'*A quiet, sleepy town in midwestern America has become the latest hot spot for Elvis fans after a sighting of the great star there last week. Since his death in 1977, literally hundreds of similar sightings have been reported ...'*

Grandad stopped and looked at Adam. 'His death?'

Adam nodded uncertainly.

'When did he die?' continued Grandad, confusion creeping across his features like a cloud covering the sun. 'I never heard anything about it. Why did nobody tell me? Eileen will be so upset. She loves Elvis ...' Grandad was becoming more and more agitated.

Adam reached over and took the paper from his trembling hands. 'It was a long time ago, Grandad. I think Nana knows already.' Grandad still looked worried. 'But we won't talk to her about it, because you're right, it'll only upset her. Let's find something else to read.' Adam quickly shuffled a few pages. 'Here!' he said enthusiastically. 'Look here, Grandad. Here's something about the football. Let's see how your team did the other day.'

But the old man had lost interest completely. Adam closed the paper and got up to put it on the central table. As he down again, his ear throbbed and he put his hand up to it.

'What's wrong with you, son?' said Grandad.

Adam shook his head and instantly regretted it. 'Ow! Sorry. Nothing. It's okay.'

But Grandad was concerned; he shifted forwards in his seat for a closer look. 'Show me.'

Reluctantly, Adam took his hand away. The ear was swollen and red, and an angry, purple bruise had already appeared at his hairline.

'In the name of ... What happened you?'

Adam sighed. He had thought Grandad wouldn't notice. 'It was a fella at school. I'm okay, Grandad. Honest.'

Granddad reached over and gently placed his huge, gnarled hand over Adam's ear. He gazed out the window and seemed, once more, to move away from the present. 'I got a thick ear once, from James Hennessy. Last week.' He rubbed his own ear thoughtfully at the memory. 'Billy told me that Hennessy's out to get me again. He's going to do it after school.'

'Why?' asked Adam softly.

The old man shrugged. 'Huh! He doesn't need a reason! He does it to everyone. But' – his voice hardened and he gripped the sides of the chair – 'he's not going to hit me again. I'm not taking it any more. I've had enough of him.'

Adam found himself nodding in agreement. *I know what that feels like*, he thought. 'What will you do, Gra – Joe?'

Grandad turned to Adam and grinned. 'I'm going to look him in the eyes, in his piggy little eyes, and I'm going to tell him: *I'm not scared of you!* Billy said that's what he did, and James legged it faster than a jackrabbit!'

The two of them smiled at the thought of James Hennessy pelting along like a frightened rabbit. In Adam's mind, James Hennessy looked suspiciously like Rory Brennan.

Maybe I need a new plan, thought Adam. *Or maybe – maybe I could use Grandad's ...*

10

DAD'S PROBLEM

Rory was clock-watching. If you'd asked him the time, he could have told you it was precisely 2.51pm. He'd been staring at the clock for ages, willing the boring minutes to pass. But they still crawled by, and he was beginning to wonder if the clock was broken. He sighed loudly.

'Get on with your work!' snapped the principal. PJ looked up to see what was going on. 'You too, Paul,' Mrs Malley told him. 'Detention ends at half three – perhaps you need some more work to do?' She began shuffling pages on her desk. 'I'm sure I have a worksheet here somewhere ...'

The three boys hurriedly bent over their work

again. Another forty minutes to go, another week on report looming, another detention at the same time next week ... They were not happy.

A small shadow flitted by the window, then landed on the sill. It was a bird, and it peered inquisitively at the shapes and shadows inside. It was right beside the desk where Adam sat, Rory noticed. Adam's starling.

* * *

'Will we go up to the shopping centre and see that new movie today?' Adam's dad asked on Saturday morning.

Adam turned away from the TV to see his dad standing behind the kitchen counter, showered and sleepy-looking, like a recently washed tortoise.

'But you were working last night, Da ... don't you have to sleep?'

'Nope, it's okay. Your mam's not feeling well, so I said I'd bring you out today. I'm grand.'

Jim didn't look grand; he had bags under his

eyes and a kind of crumpled look to his face. Adam hadn't the heart to tell him he'd already seen the film. He got up and turned off the TV. 'Okay, I'd really like that,' he said.

Adam was surprised to find that he enjoyed *Alien Empire* just as much the second time. It was great to be there with Dad, sitting companionably, sharing popcorn and sweets in the dark.

As they came out, the daylight glare of the white November sky hit Adam with an almost physical force.

'Will we walk back?' asked Dad. Adam zipped up his jacket and felt the icy wind find its way up the sleeves and through the stitches. 'Good exercise! Save the fare!' said Dad, sounding unconvinced.

They walked in silence for a few minutes before Dad spoke again.

'Listen, Adam, there's a bit of bad news.'

Adam felt an icy hand grip his stomach. What could it be? 'Is it Grandad? I haven't seen him since – since – is he okay?'

'He's fine, Adam. It's not that. It's ...'

But Adam's mind was still racing. *It must be Mam!* 'Mam?'

'Adam, Mam's fine too. She's just got a cold.'

Maybe they're splitting up. He hadn't seen Mam and Dad laughing together for ages. He knew what it was like – he'd heard about all the problems when Niamh's parents split a year ago ...

'So, anyway, the car's gone back ...' Dad was saying.

'Car?' repeated Adam.

'Yeah, the car; we can't afford to keep it, especially with Christmas coming up.'

Adam looked confused. 'I don't understand.'

Dad put his hand on Adam's shoulder. 'Have you been listening to anything I was saying?' he laughed. 'Don't worry; Mam will get another job and she'll cheer up a bit. We've got to help her and not keep asking for things or being difficult. Right?'

'You're not splitting up?' asked Adam.

Dad threw back his head and laughed. 'I knew you weren't listening, Mr Panic.' He held Adam by

'Oh, we've a few minutes to go before they join us, then.' Miss Hill tried her best to look disappointed.

At break-time Adam had to pass Rory as he went out to the yard. Rory wasn't going outside; he would be spending another break-time standing by the office.

He caught Adam by the sleeve as he passed, and leered into his face. 'Been feeding your little birdy, have you, Adam?'

Adam stopped in his tracks and glanced over at the window. Then he tried to pull free, but Rory held on long enough to give him a swift kick on the ankle. 'You're such a sap!' he spat, walking off towards the office.

Outside, Adam began to feel uneasy. Niamh and Conor were their usual cheerful selves, but Adam felt very far away from his friends. He could hear and see them, but it was as if their voices came from a long way off, as if they were actors in a film. Boys and girls ran, chased and played around him, but the noises seemed distant.

Adam's heart began thumping heavily. He didn't even hear the bell ring for the end of break. Conor had to pull him into the line. 'What's with you today, Adam? Wake up!'

The line snaked its way to the doorway and waited to be let in. There was a roaring in Adam's ears, drowning out the chat and laughter. Something was going to happen.

The children began to file into the classroom and sit down, and Miss Hill came in from the other door. Adam felt it straight away: there was something not right – some kind of atmosphere in the room. Shane and PJ were already sitting down; the principal must have sent them in early from the office. Rory was over at Adam's desk. Adam's first thought was, *What's he doing with my stuff?* Then he saw it.

His starling was inside the classroom, pecking crumbs off the inner windowsill. A small trail of crumbs led from the sill outside, right onto Adam's desk.

Suddenly Colm noticed the bird and yelled in his

booming voice, 'Miss Hill! There's a bird in the classroom.'

Startled, the starling took off. *Slam!* Rory dashed the window down.

The starling perched on a trolley, its little chest heaving, its head darting from side to side. Miss Hill said softly, 'Sit down, everyone. Try to do it quietly. Don't make any sudden movements.'

The bird suddenly noticed the window behind Miss Hill's desk. With a whoosh of feathers it flew directly towards the glass – and into it, with a sickening thud. The little creature lay stunned on the sill for a moment, then it took off again, perching on the top ledge of the blackboard. It was trembling all over, its tail-feathers vibrating with the shaking of its thin legs.

The class sat in their desks. They tried to keep still, but the bird began to dart and flit mindlessly, panic-stricken, from one side of the room to the other. *Swoop*, across someone's head, *whoosh* – up to the top corner. Somebody screamed as it swished over her shoulder; the sounds of flapping and fluttering filled the room. The noise level increased as kids began to shout suggestions: 'Close the blinds!' 'Open the windows!' 'Open the back door!' 'I'll get it, Teacher! I'll catch it!'

The starling flew, in blind terror, smack into the back window. It lay slumped again; then, unbelievably, it struggled to get up. It hopped a few metres and, with a pathetic scrabble of claws and wings, made it onto the blackboard ledge again.

Miss Hill opened the two side windows as wide as they would go, trying at the same time to quell the suggestions and the rising noise. 'Hand me that towel,' she instructed Niamh. 'If I can just get the towel over it and catch it up that way ...' she murmured, almost to herself.

All this time, Adam stood at the back door, transfixed by the sight of the terrified starling. The bird clung to the narrow ledge, with trembling claws and a heaving chest.

A light breeze came from the partly open window at the side of the classroom. The starling felt the cool air and made a last valiant dash for freedom. It crashed heavily into the glass, fell to the floor and lay still.

Miss Hill started to go over with the towel. 'Leave him!' shouted Adam, with such force that she stopped abruptly.

Adam took his jacket off and gently covered the bird, lifting it carefully and wrapping the arms of the coat softly around its tiny frame. Then he walked out the door. The whole class sat in silence, staring at him.

Outside, Adam laid the bird gently on the grass and opened the coat slightly. The little starling's head lolled back and its eyes were closed.

Adam cupped the tiny head in his hand and felt its impossible lightness. He stroked the soft feathers on the bird's neck and chest. They were so soft, he could hardly feel them against his fingertips. Up close, Adam could see every colour. He wondered how he could ever have thought that the starling was just plain brown. The colour was more like – like petrol, the beautiful colour of petrol spilled on a path: greens, blues, a faint sheen of silver ... A breeze ruffled the tiny feathers on his starling's head, giving it the impish, scruffy look it had had the first time Adam had seen it.

Niamh came quietly down the path and took his arm. 'Come on, Adam,' she said gently. 'Miss Hill sent me. You have to come in.'

Adam stood up.

'It may live; it might only be stunned,' she said uncertainly.

Adam said nothing. He turned and began to stride back up the path.

'Wait!' called Niamh, trying to catch up with him. But he was too quick. With a loud slam, Adam burst in through the door of the classroom and looked around wildly. The kids were all sitting at their desks; Miss Hill was trying to keep everyone calm.

Adam marched over to Shane and PJ and, in one movement, swept everything from their desks and sent it crashing onto the floor. Then he turned and strode up to Rory, who was ashen-faced.

Adam took a small step backwards, raised his foot and kicked Rory's desk harder than he'd ever kicked anything in his life. The desk careered across the floor with a satisfyingly loud scraping noise, teetered on two legs for a moment, and then came smashing down, tipping all its contents to the floor in a muddled heap. No one spoke. No one moved.

Adam looked straight at Rory, swallowing a lump in his throat. 'What did he ever do to you?' he asked. 'What did that starling ever do to you?' he was shouting now. 'It's just a little bird. It's just a – a creature! It flies around. It pecks up crumbs in the yard. What does it do to you? What does it do that makes you hate it, Rory?'

He was so full of rage and strength, he couldn't stand still. He stamped down the length of the classroom, his anger like a boiling liquid trying to burst out of his skin. He grabbed a box full of pens and pencils and flung it wildly to the floor.

'And what did I ever do to you, Rory?' he shouted. 'I've never done anything to you. Never! And I didn't sneak on you, either. It was someone else.'

At the memory of the bin and Niall, Adam almost lost his courage. He could still remember the stench in that bin, and the awful fear …. His eyes stung, but he fought it and carried on.

'You're the sap, Rory! You smash everything. You hate everything! But I'll tell you something.' He paused, then said slowly and deliberately, 'I'm not scared of you any more.'

Adam stood completely still in the middle of the room, startled by his own words. He looked at the pinched, petrified face of Rory Brennan, at his eyes darting all over the room.

A tiny smile appeared at the corner of Adam's mouth. He took a deep breath. *'I'm not scared of you!'* he yelled.

Adam walked slowly up to Rory, bringing his face so close that their noses were almost touching. 'I'm not scared of you any more, Rory,' he finished quietly. Then he turned and walked out the door.

Miss Hill had moved over near Rory's desk, just in case. She had thought about intervening –

maybe bringing the boys into the office – but there
had been no need.

She watched Adam close the classroom door
with a firm click, and then turned to look at Rory.
His mouth hung open in shock and disbelief.

Good on you, Adam, Miss Hill thought with a
tiny spark of happiness. *He had it coming.*

12

RUNNING

It began as a faint rustling sound, a kind of crackly buzzing, like bad reception on a radio. It rushed in through Adam's ears and swiftly filled his head until it was like having his own personal tornado in his brain. At first, Adam thought the noise was the wind in the trees that surrounded the school; but as he walked steadily down the path and out the school gate, the sound grew louder and louder – rustling changed into roaring.

Adam broke into a run. No one was chasing him, and he didn't even know where he was going – he just had to run. Down to the corner, up over the bank, across the main road ... House, house, shop, shop, house – his feet pounded the pavement and his mind beat to the rhythm. Bus stop, shop, house, house ... On and on, past the roundabout, over the main road – lights, park gate, house, house ...

Slowly, it dawned on Adam where he was running. To Grandad.

Plenty of soccer with Danny had made Adam fairly fit, but, even so, he had no idea where the energy for this marathon run was coming from. His mam always drove them to visit Grandad; Adam had never asked how far it was, but it took about ten minutes in the car. Today, he knew he could run all the way to the hospital. Something about the pounding of his feet on the pavement calmed him, made him feel better.

Adam slowed to a steady jog and kept going. As long as he was running, he felt no pain.

When he reached the hospital gate, he forced himself to stop running. His legs were trembling, his lungs squeezed to the point of collapse. He leaned against the gate and hung his head, gasping.

Gradually the gasps subsided, and he straightened up. Leaning back against the cool metal, he listened to his own breathing as it slowed to a normal pace. He could go in now.

* * *

In the ward, the patients sat gathered around the central table, which was set for their main meal. A nurse had said Adam could go in and sit with his grandfather while he ate.

Birdy was sitting at the head of the table, tweeting frantically. The old lady who normally guarded the TV remote still had it in her hands; with shaking fingers, she pointed the gadget at Birdy and began pressing buttons. 'Why won't it work?' she asked the woman beside her. 'I can't turn it off.'

Still Birdy whistled.

'How are you, Birdy?' said Adam.

'Tweet-tweet, tweet-tweet!' he replied.

Adam drew up a chair and sat down beside Grandad, who hadn't looked up. He was staring intently at the empty plate in front of him.

'Hi, Grandad!' said Adam, giving his arm a gentle squeeze.

The old man still didn't look up. With some effort, he picked up his knife and fork, though the food hadn't yet been served. Adam noticed how huge his grandad's hands were still, though the skin that covered them seemed as thin as clingfilm and almost as transparent – he could see red and blue veins, and the stringy sinews that wrapped the giant knuckles and bones. Working as a mechanic on the buses, Grandad had used his hands to earn his living, and now they were living proof of his life's work. Adam remembered that Grandad had always called his hands 'shovels' – he said they were made of asbestos. Adam didn't know what asbestos was, but he reckoned it must be heatproof – Grandad had said that whenever he held anything hot.

Now, the knife and fork looked tiny in the huge gnarled hands. Grandad began to cut at the surface of the plate. The metal clattered and clashed on the empty china.

'What are you doing there, Grandad?' Adam asked.

Grandad stared even harder at the plate and tried again. 'Darn it! This is fierce tough meat!' he exclaimed. 'What are they feeding us in this hotel? I asked for salmon!' he said in disgust. 'That looks more like a sprat – and it's as tough as an old boot. I can't cut it!'

'But you haven't got any f–' Adam began; then he noticed the picture on the plate. It showed a leaping fish, and there were tiny fishes decorating the edge of the china. He stifled a giggle and took hold of the plate. 'It's okay, Grandad. I'll go and get you another one.'

By now the dinner ladies had arrived with the trolley and were ladling stew onto plates. Adam went over to them, carrying his grandad's tough fish. 'Be sure you tell them how tough it was!' called Grandad. 'They shouldn't serve stuff like that. Don't let them away with it! Desperate hotel, this! We're checking out as soon as Eileen gets back from her shopping.'

After dinner which Grandad had eaten merrily
– once his tough fish was replaced – Adam and the
old man sat by the window in their usual places.
Adam needed to tell Grandad about the awful
morning. He needed to say it aloud.

'Grandad? I had this bird ...'

'Bird?' echoed Grandad.

'Sort of like a pet bird. You know – tweet-
tweet, like Birdy over there.' Birdy's bright eyes
twinkled, and he tweeted obligingly in their
direction.

Adam looked closely at his grandad's worn
features. 'Anyway, a guy at school – Rory – he
played a trick, and ...' Adam paused, not sure if
this made any sense to Grandad.

'A mean trick,' said Grandad, with some feeling.

'Yes!' cried Adam. 'Rory played a mean trick
and the bird, my starling, is ... is dead.'

Grandad seemed to have absorbed that. 'Dead?
Ah, no!' he cried.

Adam carried on, encouraged by the fact that
Grandad seemed to be following. 'So I went up to

Rory and I yelled at him and I kicked all his stuff around.'

'A fight?'

'Yeah, I suppose. Sort of like a fight. Then I walked out of the place,' Adam said.

The old man was nodding and smiling. 'That's right!' he exclaimed.

Adam waited. Grandad put out one huge, bony hand and patted Adam's knee. 'I love birds!' he said, looking directly at his grandson.

'I know you do, Grandad. So do –'

'You shouldn't hurt them, you know.' He spoke over Adam's words. 'Don't let anyone hurt you, son. And don't let them hurt the birds.' Birdy gave an extra-loud chirp in agreement.

'Now, when are they serving dinner in this place?' demanded Grandad. 'I'm starving.'

* * *

Getting back home was a bit more difficult than getting to the hospital had been. Adam found a pound coin in his jeans pocket and got a bus most of the way. He knew Mam wouldn't be back yet, and he was relieved to find his house-keys in the same pocket as the money.

As he reached home, he glanced up automatically at the drainpipe; then, with a wrench, he realised what he had been looking for. He let himself in, went upstairs and lay face-down on the bed. He was exhausted. No tears came. No feelings. Nothing. Adam slept.

He was dimly aware of doors opening and closing, the phone ringing, voices. But still he slept on.

'No, I'll talk to him.' Dad's voice outside his bedroom door brought Adam fully awake. It was almost dusk, and the room was cold.

Dad came in and sat on the bed. He glanced at Adam and gave a chuckle. 'You're something!'

Adam scanned his face, trying to read his emotions – was he angry? Did he know what had happened?

'Well, you told them, Adam. You certainly did! You say nothing for months, but when you decide to, you sure let them have it.'

Adam didn't know where to start. He sat up in bed, shivering in the cool evening.

'Dad, I –' he began.

'Listen, Adam,' said Dad, giving his knee a squeeze, 'I think you did the right thing. Well, you shouldn't have run off, of course, but you did the right thing by standing up for yourself.'

Adam gave a wan smile.

'Why don't we get you something to eat? You'll need your strength – we've to go to the principal in the morning. The three of us!' Dad laughed as he left the bedroom. 'I'd better find me a clean jacket!' he said from the stairs.

Adam heard the stairs creak, then a pause. 'Oh, yeah, that reminds me,' Dad said. 'Some girl phoned. Said to tell you your jacket was empty – whatever that means.' He carried on down the stairs.

Empty! Oh! Maybe ... Adam lay in the dark and dared to hope. When he'd walked out of school, he hadn't passed the place where he'd laid the starling. Remembering, Adam realised he hadn't even looked in that direction – hadn't let himself look. Maybe now he could allow himself to hope. He would balance the sickening memory of the flailing wings, the terrified fluttering, with the tiny hope that the starling had recovered.

All night long, these two thoughts wrestled in Adam's mind. Finally, only an hour before he was going to have to get up, Adam fell into a deep sleep – hoping.

13

SORRY

On the way to school in the car, Deirdre drilled Adam in Apology Technique, terrified that he would be suspended or even expelled. 'Don't try anything smart, Adam!' Her fingers clenched on the steering-wheel as she accelerated. 'I mean it. You're in enough trouble ...' She braked suddenly to avoid a cyclist. Dad turned and gave Adam the thumbs-up.

'I won't, Mam.'

'Just say –' she began.

'I know, sorry. I'll just say I'm sorry,' Adam droned, like a parrot.

Jim patted Deirdre's arm. 'He'll be fine, love.

It'll all be fine. That is, if we live long enough to meet the woman. Slow down!' Nerves always made Mam drive fast. She sighed a long sigh and slowed down a little.

Adam looked out the window at the grey sky – the empty grey sky.

* * *

Adam's parents looked strangely out of place in the principal's office, sitting bolt upright in the visitors' chairs with Adam between them, as the early-morning business of school bustled outside. Deirdre was biting her lip and picking at her fingernails, while Jim shifted uncomfortably in the hard chair.

No one spoke while Mrs Malley finished reading the pages in front of her. With a sudden lurch of nerves, Adam realised that the report she was reading was about him. He recognised Miss Hill's distinctive sloping handwriting. He quickly looked away – he didn't want to look as if he was trying to read what it said.

He found himself looking out the window, where a succession of curious children passed by, craning their necks to see what was going on in the office. Adam was already a minor celebrity for standing up to Rory. He would be a living legend for walking out of school without permission.

When, at last, Mrs Malley spoke, it was clear that Adam was not in quite as much trouble as they had all feared.

'Adam,' she began, 'I am not going to hold you entirely responsible for yesterday's events.' Mam and Dad looked at each other questioningly, and Adam glanced rapidly from one to the other.

The principal continued, 'I have spoken to Miss Hill and other members of staff, and it's only now that I'm realising the full extent of the pressure you've been under.' She sighed. 'Perhaps, if you'd spoken to one of us, we could have helped you' – she peered sternly at Adam – 'rather than letting matters get out of hand.'

Deirdre was nodding vigorously. She began, 'We told him to tell the teacher –'

'Quite,' replied Mrs Malley. 'That would have been the best course of action, but, at any rate, let's hope things have now been resolved.' She turned to Jim. 'He'll be on report, of course, for three days, because he left the premises without permission; but there'll be no further punishment. I think – indeed, we all think – that he's had more than enough.'

* * *

And that was that. Adam walked into class afterwards, not quite sure if he was the good guy or the bad guy. As he took his place, there was whispering and murmuring, but Miss Hill smiled cheerily at him and Niamh gave him a thumbs-up. Rory sat looking down at his desk, scared to meet Adam's gaze. Shane and PJ grinned foolishly, like a pair of idiotic hamsters. Conor looked up and smiled. 'Welcome back, Adam,' he said.

* * *

At break, Adam was kicking a football around

with Niamh, Conor, and some of the others. One side of the pitch backed onto the grass verge of the main road, with spiked railings separating the two areas of green. In the distance, Adam saw the tall, rangy figure of Danny crossing the road.

He made his way over to the railings and put his long arm towards Adam. 'Put it there, me boyo!' he demanded.

Adam stared.

'Put it there! Shake! I want to shake the hand of the man who scared the living daylights out of Rory Brennan!' Danny's knuckly hand still hung in mid-air.

Adam smiled sheepishly. 'Did Mam tell you?'

'Nope! It's all over town, amigo! I saw him and his brother up at the shopping centre yesterday afternoon. Their ma was in a shop, and she made the two of them stand outside holding the trolley. I heard them talking about you as I went past.' Danny shook his head and gave a long, dramatic whistle. 'I don't think they'll be messing with you any more, my friend. Not with your reputation!'

Adam looked suspicious. 'Reputation?'

Danny grinned, stretched his arm in a bit further and punched Adam on the shoulder. 'You're a hard man now, Adam. They were quaking in their little shiny shoes! What was it they said about you?' He scratched his head for effect. 'Anyway, I think "wild" and "mad" were some of the words used ...' He turned and began walking off, then looked back. 'Madman Adam ... what do you think? I like the sound of it. I'd stick with that one!'

Adam grinned.

Niamh and Conor came over to the railings. They watched Danny cross the road, where he turned and saluted before walking off.

The three friends walked over to their tree and sat down, leaning against its rough bark. 'Are you okay after yesterday?' Conor asked. 'It was really terrible watching that little bird, wasn't it?'

Adam nodded.

'Listen, Adam,' said Niamh. 'I think the bird is alive. Your jacket was empty when I came out after school. Maybe it was just stunned for a while and then it got better.'

Adam scanned the skyline. He looked out past the houses, the main road, the grey hills, the white winter sky. No sign of any birds.

'And another thing – I'm sorry I didn't believe you when you told me about the bird following you ...'

'It's okay,' Adam interrupted.

'No, it's not. I'm sorry. It's just so hard to imagine a bird following you – being so tame and everything ...' Niamh fiddled with the end of one of her long plaits.

'Niamh,' said Adam, 'really, it's okay. Maybe he was following me, maybe he wasn't. I suppose I won't ever know.' He drew up his knees and rested his head on them. Niamh and Conor exchanged worried glances.

Suddenly, Adam jumped up and peered at the school. It was hard to tell from where he stood, but it looked as if there was something perched on the gable end of the building. A small shadow that, even from this distance, looked like a starling – a small and particularly scruffy starling.

'Would you look at that!' cried Adam, turning towards Niamh and Conor.

'What?' they said together, just as the bell rang to signal the end of break.

'Up there!' he cried, pointing.

All three of them followed Adam's outstretched finger, but the bird had gone.

'It doesn't matter,' said Adam. Then he flashed a sudden grin. 'It doesn't matter – come on, let's go in.'

More RED FLAG books from the O'Brien Press

THE GREAT PIG ESCAPE
Linda Moller

When the farm cat tells Runtling the pig of his approaching fate, this little piggy realises that the trip to market is one he must avoid at all costs. He warns his twelve pig-mates and together they escape. They find an abandoned farm, but then new owners arrive and the pigs fear that their escape has been in vain. But Nick and Polly Faraway have strange, alternative ideas about farming and a lifestyle that might work to the benefit of pigs and humans. Maybe there can be a happy ending after all!

COWS ARE VEGETARIANS

Siobh«n Parkinson

Michelle lives in the town. When she visits her country cousins, Sinéad and Dara, she is not impressed by farm life. She finds wild animals in the garden, lambs in the kitchen, muck everywhere and no shops or street lights. Sinéad and Dara may laugh at her city ways, but how on earth is Michelle going to put up with all this? And, more importantly, how on earth are Sinéad and Dara going to put up with Michelle?

THE FIGHT FOR PLOVER HILL
Eilís Dillon

John and his grandfather, Old Dan, are the only people living on Plover Hill, a little farm cut off from the rest of the valley by floodwater. They have eggs from their ducks and hens, milk and butter from the cows, and in the woods live every kind of animal and bird you ever saw: foxes, hedgehogs, squirrels, rabbits and, of course, plover. But a local property developer has his eye on Plover Hill – it would make a fine place to bring shooting parties. He challenges Dan's right to the land. Will John be able to save Plover Hill for his grandfather and for the animals for whom it is a sanctuary?

LEPRECHAUN ON THE LOOSE

Annette Kelleher

Biddy Blatherskate is fed up with wet weather and minding her father's gold. When Corey, a young Australian boy visiting Ireland, stumbles on her treasure, she's willing to do a deal in exchange for a chance to visit Australia. Her father's gold for Corey's passport! But leprechauns and humans don't mix – not without a heap of trouble for all concerned! Sunburnt and in hiding, Biddy is soon fed up with Australia, too. Meanwhile, Corey's spending spree comes to nothing because no one will accept little pieces of gold instead of money. Things are looking grim for Biddy and Corey ...

WOLFGRAN
Finbar O'Connor

Granny has sold her house to the three little pigs and moved into the Happy-Ever-After Home for Retirement Characters from Fairy Tales. But the Big Bad Wolf is still on her trail! Disguised as a little old lady, the wolf is causing mayhem as he prowls the city streets, swallowing anybody who gets in his way, including several very polite policemen. Hot on his heels are Chief Inspector Plonker, Sergeant Snoop and a very clever little Girl Guide in a red hood. But will they get to the wolf before he gets to Granny?

WOLFGRAN RETURNS
Finbar O'Connor

Inspector Plonker is once more on the trail of his old enemy, Wolfgran, but this time he's going undercover. Disguised in a pantomime wolf suit, can the Inspector and his faithful sidekick Sergeant Snoop escape being throttled by Granny Riding Hood's nephew, blasted by the Chief of Police, hand-bagged by a bus queue full of very cranky old ladies and run over by the terrifying vets from TV's 'Pet Patrol'? And will they manage to stop the Big Bad Wolf before he gets to the Grand Gala Bingo Night and finally makes a meal of Little Red Riding Hood?

ALBERT AND THE MAGICIAN
Leon McAuley

When the headmaster announces that The Great Gazebo is coming to visit the school, Albert's big sister, Fionnuala, tells him awful tales about the powers of magicians, especially over seven-year-old boys. Poor Albert is terrified! When a funny-looking old man turns up at the school gate on an old banger of a bike, Albert kindly helps him carry his bags – then, horror of horrors, he discovers that this is the magician … and now he has a *special interest in Albert!*

WALTER SPEAZLEBUD

David Donohue

Walter Speazlebud is a whizz at spelling backwards. While the other children in his class struggle to remember their spellings *forwards*, Walter can rattle off any word *backwards*. But Walter has an even better gift: the power of **Noitanigami** (Imagination). That means he can make people, and animals, go backwards in time. Walter inherited both skills from his favourite person: his grandfather. So when his horrible teacher, Mr Strong, starts picking on Walter, he had better watch out. And so had the even more horrible class bully, Danny Biggles. Because when Speazlebud's about, it spells **elbuort** (trouble) for all bullies …

Also by Gillian Perdue, for beginner readers

CONOR'S COWBOY SUIT

When Conor gets a cowboy suit he is very happy. 'Yee haw!' he says. 'Stick 'em up!' All night he has cowboy dreams. Conor's suit is the best thing ever. But can he wear it to school?

CONOR'S CONCERT

Conor is learning the piano. But the tunes he must practise are boring. Conor wants to play something exciting. He makes up his own very special music. But will it do for the concert?

**Send for our full-colour catalogue
or check out our website**